HOW TO
OUTSMART
YOUR CAT

How to Outsmart Your Cat by Bill Helmer

ISBN: 978-1-949790-74-0 (pbk)

ISBN: 978-1-949790-75-7 (ebk)

Layout by Bill Helmer and Mark Givens

First Pelekinesis Printing 2022

For information:

Pelekinesis, 112 Harvard Ave #65, Claremont, CA 91711 USA

Library of Congress Cataloging-in-Publication Data

Names: Helmer, William J, 1936- author.
Title: How to outsmart your cat / by Bill Helmer.
Description: Claremont, CA : Pelekinesis, [2022] | Summary: "Legions of
   American cat owners will welcome this manual, the first ever to speak
   out frankly on a difficult subject that one's sense of embarrassment
   usually consigns to some small dark closet of the mind where one's
   mistakes are concealed. In this case, the mistake is having fallen in
   love with a kitten for its cuteness, playfulness, and affection that
   seem to promise years of pleasure and amusement. Only a reluctance to
   admit that one was wrong, that one was taken in by a wily lower animal,
   deters many people from admitting the truth and giving the animal (plus
   a can of cat food) to the first urchin who happens by. Correcting this
   problem and saving the relationship is the purpose of this program,
   which requires only determination on the part of the cat's owner. It
   will require a bit more on the part of the cat"-- Provided by publisher.

Identifiers: LCCN 2022027503 (print) | LCCN 2022027504 (ebook) | ISBN
   9781949790740 (paperback) | ISBN 9781949790757 (ebook)
Subjects: LCSH: Cats--Miscellanea. | Cats--Behavior--Humor.
Classification: LCC SF446.5 .H456 2022 (print) | LCC SF446.5 (ebook) |
   DDC 636.8/0887--dc23/eng/20220628
LC record available at https://lccn.loc.gov/2022027503
LC ebook record available at https://lccn.loc.gov/2022027504

www.pelekinesis.com

HOW TO
OUTSMART
YOUR CAT

*The Puss 'n Boot Camp: A Tough Love Program To
Reinvest Your Feline Friend With Entertainment Value*

by Bill Helmer

Idle hands are the devil's workshop.

For Jan Lee Rekemeyer
and Her Kind

Nature endowed kittens with enough cuteness and playfulness to ensure species survival and let it go at that. This helped the creature advance from mouser to house pet. Once tenured, however, a cat relaxes. It abandons the qualities that once made it lovable and adopts airs of independence, finickiness, and entitlement that leave us feeling swindled—the victims of a promise not kept.

This manual explores the problem and shows how you can reinvest your cat with entertainment value.

—Doctor Horace Naismith

Frank Stack

CONTENTS

Vol. 3 — No. 5   January 29, 1985   55c

Sun

Desperate citizens flee in terror as ...

GIANT FLYING CAT TERRIFIES STATE

Cure backache just by rubbing on your head

BIZARRE SCANDAL OF AMERICA'S GAY WRESTLERS

Thousands of truckers to get tax refunds

DOES YOUR WIFE SPEND FOOD MONEY TO BUY ROMANCE?

Magic power of dollar sign can make you rich

NEW BLOOD TEST PREDICTS IF YOUR MARRIAGE WILL LAST

Garlic restores faded sex life

SICKO TORTURES HOOKERS WITH TRAINED ROACHES

If you thought Boy George was strange, LOOK AT THIS!

PSY-CATHERAPY

YOUR CAT AND ITS COUNSELING

Does your cat sleep twenty hours a day?
Does your cat sleep where it is not supposed to?
Does your cat show affection only when hungry?
Does your cat turn up its nose at dry cat food?
Does your cat understand nothing you tell it?
Does your cat appear to be untrainable?
Does your cat appear to be intractable?
Does your cat seem incredibly stupid?

If the answer to any of these questions is *Yes*, your cat is perfectly normal.

If, however, your cat is cranky or aggressive, refuses to poop in its litter-box, to purr properly, or sleeps standing up, it is possible that your cat is not a cat but some other fur-bearing animal and you should have it checked out by a veterinarian.

Animal psychotherapy is a new field in which the practitioner seeks to determine the source of your pet's conflicts, depression, anxiety, and panic attacks and to help it *work things out.* Some pet psycho-therapists treat dogs but not cats, whose resistance to therapy makes them the animal

1

equivalent of the alcoholic. Dogs possess a sense of Original Sin that gives them an eagerness to please, but cats are either not so burdened or are heavily into denial.

One school of cat psychotherapy holds that your pet's happiness will be enhanced through a combination of desensitization, aversion stimuli, and positive reinforcement—the stick-and-carrot approach.

Another school of cat psychotherapy (I think it's the Freudian one) holds that declining playfulness and diminished affection are symptoms of depression, and that depression in animals as in man results from anger turned inward. What our Puss 'n Boot Camp should do is give the cat something to be angry *about*.

There is also a method favored by those few therapists who enjoy the challenge presented by cats. It is called INSTAFIX®.

INSTAFIX THERAPY

INSTAFIX® is an eclectic system developed by Doctor Horace Naismith, EMT,[1] owner of the Good Neighbor Marriage Counseling Clinic and Surpentarium where he offers a Discount Divorce[2] and practices "Psycatrology."[3]

The secret of INSTAFIX®, according to the Doctor (Doctor being his first name), is to first tell the owners of a neurotic cats that they should have their animal "put down and stuffed" so it can live forever in their memory. The fact that the walls of his clinic are decorated with mounted cat heads (all roadkill) hanging between old *Playboy* calendars and pictures

---

1. Emergency Marital Technician.
2. Which he calls "The wrecking ball of progress."
3. The Doctor has a thing for coining words.

of Jesus, convinces most cat owners that the doctor is nuts—until they learn that this is a deliberate misrepresentation intended to bring owner and cat closer together in the face of a common enemy.

The author of this manual will incorporate some elements of INSTAFIX® because it puts Doctor Naismith at the cutting edge of animal psychiatrics and qualifies him to serve as our consultant, which has nothing to do with his possession of the author's diaries and other information of a sensitive nature.

SOME PRELIMINARIES

First of all, if we are contending with a cat that has lost its entertainment value, we want to restore the romp and frolic that endeared it in the first place. That is the primary purpose of our Puss 'n Boot Camp. When a once playful kitten enters adolescence and becomes a rebellious, ungrateful, arrogant, sarcastic teenager, it will benefit from enrollment in what amounts to a military school. Likewise, our Puss 'n Boot Camp will help our juvenile overcome its delinquency, and if our cat has aged into slothfulness, it will help it appreciate its easy life by making it a little less so.

Think back. During grade school you no doubt had a teacher that you loved to hate. To an older generation, she was the Bitch of Buchenwald, he old Shit-For-Brains. This is the teacher who gave you tough homework assignments, took off for bad spelling, rejected your excuses, and possessed a finely-tuned bullshit detector. She or he made you learn stuff you would never use, crippling your social life.

But in later years you had to admit that this pedagogue was also pretty good, for she or he taught you not just facts (which come in handy at cocktail parties) but the self-discipline it takes to learn, to perform, to excel. The same is needed by your cat. We want to be able to say,

THIS HURTS ME MORE THAN IT DOES YOU

Just as a doctor must not flinch at the sight of blood, we must not fail to do what has to be done. If this duty is not *unpleasant*, if one *likes* to abuse one's cat, then one must consider the possibility that one is merely *sadistic*. But not if we feel Owner Guilt. Owner Guilt cannot be experienced by a sadist. We experience Owner Guilt because we *care* about our cat, know that our cat *needs* us, and know that we can help our cat recover the *entertainment value* it lost through our own neglect. That is True Love, and True Love has no strings attached. Maybe a few strings. We don't want to visit our own problems upon our cat, of course, but if your once-cute pussy slumbers pathetically and glowers when disturbed, these traits may be a *cry for help*.

Stray cat's lives run out as it cuts power to 3 cities

A wayward cat knocked out electrical power in the cities of Redondo, Manhattan Beach and Hermosa Beach yesterday when it crept into a Southern California Edison substation and caused a

Help, of course, lends itself to interpretation. We can "help" a youngster by showing him how to do something or how to do something better. For our cat there is a different technique: you sneak up on its blind side and trick it into compliance.

This compliance should not derive from fear. As FDR once put it, *The only thing we have to fear is fear itself.* So your cat should not cringe at the prospect of brutality or quiver at a scowl of disapproval. We should begin our training program only after we have taken what we will call the Hippocatic Oath:

FIRST, DO NO HARM

Of course some cats, like alcoholics, may have to hit bottom before they turn around. Then it's one day at a time. If your cat goes off the wagon, it will be a test of your resolve. You are its Sponsor, after all, and if you weaken you will lose your cat's respect. Only when your cat has recognized its faults, has been saved from itself, and is showing signs of recovery, will it beam up at you as if to say,

THANKS! I NEEDED THAT!

But we're getting ahead of ourselves. We need to calm down and realize that our kitty-cat is more petworthy than, say, a 'possum or an aardvark; that it may have ripened but has not yet gone to seed. So let us be inspired by this little poem, which appeared in the January 1928 issue of *Harper's* magazine.

TO A CAT, PURRING
by Florence S. Small

PANSY-FACE and raspberry-paws,
Hidden thorns are these your claws;
Moist and cool is your tiny nose
As tight-knit bud of a hedge wild rose.
Sleek as a crow's wing, back and side;
Green as a leek, your eyes, and wide
With diamond and mysterious stare;
The treacherous tiger slumbers there.
So still, you dream, and your whiskers stir;
You purr and purr and purr and purr.
With breath as soft as a shadow's wing,
You think of killings when you sing.

Wasn't that nice?

But before we get to our Puss'n Boot Camp, we should acknowledge that our cat, over many centuries, has had its ups and downs.

A BRIEF HISTORY OF CATS

Thou art the Great Cat, the avenger of the Gods, and the judge of worlds, and the president of the sovereign chiefs and the governor of the Holy Circle; thou art indeed the Great Cat.

— Inscription on the Royal Tombs at Thebes

In spite of the veneration which the Egyptians had for the cat, we are told that the punishment for adultery by a woman in Egypt was to be sewn into a sack with a live cat and flung into the Nile.

— Mildred Kirk

IN THE BEGINNING

So many cultural, social, political, civil, and religious things started in Mesopotamia that one would not be far wrong in speculating that Mesopotamians domesticated the cat (you read it here first).

Actually, one could be several thousand miles and a few millennia wrong without it making any difference to cats, so we'll go with Mesopotamia. And we'll speculate that this took place when the Sumerians, after establishing the first independent city-states in Mesopotamia, conducted weird breeding experiments that yielded a small, slothful runt of the feline species that slept a lot. This must have occurred sometime before Mesopotamia was dominated by the tyrants who, in 539 BC, got their lands absorbed by the Persian Empire, and *blah, blah, blah.* We got tired of Googling before there was any mention of cats, so I'm sure a lot was left out. But we did consult some two dozen cat books and histories dating back to 1920, so a lot of this is true.

Anyway, the Egyptians were the first to take the cat seriously. Probably they looked at our Mesopotamian Cat, declared that *they* had domesticated it, and then treated it like royalty, as do cat fanciers today. Egyptian cat owners even formed cults that competed with one another so vigorously the animal became venerated,

Berserk pet cat attacks 8-yr.-old girl!

An 8-year-old girl was viciously clawed, bitten and slashed when her family's pet cat mysteriously went haywire — and attacked the child in her own house!

Amy Johnson's dad Mike managed to knock the spanking cat off the girl with a broomstick. Then he strangled it to prevent another attack.

But the girl's mother is terrified that little Amy has been scarred both physically and emotionally for life.

"She was screaming and

The only way to stop it was to strangle it, says dad

eye that took four stitches to close.

The bizarre drama began when the Johnson's 8-year-old ran

then worshiped, and finally placed at the head of the hierarchy of animal-gods. That was about 2000 BC.

The cat cult capital was called Bubastis and there the creature was consecrated as Bastet, the goddess with the head of a cat. Bastet was also a fashion statement for Egyptian women who wished to resemble the cat-goddess in her "slanting eyes, supple loins, noble bearing and inscrutable gaze," according to one historian. He also said that illustrations of the cat reached their zenith in tombs built during the reign of Amen Hotep III.[4]

Egypt's holy cats were treated like sacred cows. The death of one required lamentation and mourning, and the deliberate killing of one was punishable by death, which even the modern day cat owner might consider extreme.

In 608 BC, somebody called Necho defeated somebody called Josiah, king of Judah, in the Battle of Megiddo, by arming his troops with cats that were whirled overhead to howl like Stuka dive bombers. The soldiers also used them as razor-clawed cudgels and hurled them, grenade-style, at the thoroughly

---

4. I would guess that Egyptian men who hustled Egyptian women who had slanting eyes, supple loins, etc., were said to be tombcatting around. (Little joke there.)

How to Outsmart Your Cat

rattled defenders. Such tactics must have convinced the conquered Josiah that he was dealing with real nut cases.

And about 500 BC the Persian forces attacking Pelusium encountered fierce resistance from the Egyptians and were about to say the hell with it until their leader, Cambyses, came up with a brilliant tactic. Knowing the Egyptians were queer for cats, he ordered his soldiers to capture every one they could find, drape themselves with the animals like some kind of Kevlar, and then wade into the defenders. When the Egyptians realized they couldn't land a blow without bashing a cat, they hung it up and the Persians prevailed.

Pacemaker keeps kitty purring

Only 3 other cats in world have device

Shy-Anne the Siamese cat is as frisky as a kitten despite her 15 years — since surgeons perked up her troubled ticker with a pacemaker.

The spunky pussycat is one of four felines in the world to survive the delicate operation — and the oldest.

Her veterinarians said Shy-Anne's chances of surviving without a pacemaker were

The use of these battlecats, as I will call them, ended with the Peloponnesian War (431-404 BC), fought between the rival Greek city-states of Sparta and Athens. After the surrender of Athens and the fall of Greek civilization, cats re-emerged as objects of veneration and were consecrated to the goddess Diana. The Arabs even worshiped a "golden cat," which didn't do much for the creature's humility. But it also tells of a sect, the Mystic Brotherhood of Siddi Heddi, that went so far as to fatten cats and feast on them as part of an annual if fairly disgusting ritual.[5] Some years later the Aryans discovered a market for cats in Continental Europe. There, cat pelts were a coveted material for making cold-weather gear for those who wore cats instead of worshiping them.[6]

---

5. Vestiges of this survive in fancy foreign restaurants patronized by quiche-eaters.

6. It is not known what the Aryans did with cat skeletons and innards, unless those are what inspired dogs to become "man's best friend."

Its changing status from deity to commodity probably accounts for the cat's own change of attitude. With the "protected species" concept far in the future, they may have decided that the demand for cat pelts required making themselves useful with their fur still in place.

CHURCH VS. CATS

After the birth of Jesus, the Christians first tried to ignore cats and kick Muslim butt in a series of Crusades. These efforts were less than successful, and the fifth attempt, the Children's Crusade (1212), failed miserably.[7] But when cat idolatry began to flourish in competition with the Savior, a pope or two hired Dark Age theologians to associate cats with evil, which only ran their price up.

Nun strangles cat

A Roman Catholic nun was fined $500 for strangling a kitten that mewed too loudly at night.
Sister Franziska Lekse of Graz, Austria, admitted strangling the kitten with a cord after being told she couldn't keep it in the convent because it mewed too loudly.
The 57-year-old nun said she

The "evil" business suited Pre-Renaissance engineers who had modified an earlier weapon (invented by Dionysus the Elder) into great wheeled machines made of wood, iron, and hemp. These could hurl objects in the manner of a giant sling-shot, and because some of these shots included cats (that's true!), the contraptions became known as *cat*apults.

I'm not sure about the catapult thing, but I do know that large batches of cats were in fact launched over the walls of fortifications to occupy the defenders while battering rams were brought to bear. Early animal-protectionists eventually halted the military use of cats, rams, and bears, much to the dismay of rock-protectionists, who vainly protested the loading of

---

7. Some claim that kittens were used to recruit the child-soldiers, most of whom either died en route to the Holy Land or were captured and enslaved by the Muslims. A few may have been freed on the condition they tend to the kittens and empty their litter-boxes, but Muslim grownups soon found they had to do that themselves and decided that cat-care was what the Christians had in mind all along.

How to Outsmart Your Cat

catapults with boulders.[8]

During the Middle Ages, as cats were increasingly disparaged by the Roman Catholic Church, the more valued they became to pagans and Satanists, just to upset the Catholics.

CAT IS ORDAINED MINISTER

A PRETTY KITTY has found a higher calling in life than chasing mice and playing with string — he's now an ordained minister!

If any congregation is interested, Reverend Teddy is available to perform services, marriages and baptisms — while keeping the church rodent-free.

Teddy, a calico cat, recently received his preacher's credentials from the United Christian Church and Ministerial A°.

Kathleen decided to check it out by trying to sign up Teddy, her cat. All it took was $20 cash and Teddy became the world's first meowing minister, with a certificate to prove it.

While she didn't exactly state that Teddy was a cat, Kathleen did provide some unusual information on the application.

For Teddy's birth date she put April 2, 1989. Where it asked for the applicant's calling to the ministry, she ·····

In the 15th Century, the pagan cults of Holda and Freyia practiced rites in which one goddess was supposed to appear in a chariot drawn by twenty black cats, while another black cat would be leading a cortege of virgins either riding on tomcats or disguised in their skins. These "adepts," as they were called, would work themselves into a lather by "screaming and howling before giving themselves over to orgiastic reveling."

By this time witchcraft was in full flower, catching blame for bad luck, bad judgment, bad everything, even plagues, and the Church made use of that superstition whenever it contradicted its teachings. This only fostered more Devil worship, of course, for any woman who acted a little screwy was suspected of witchcraft. Oddly enough, a few of these ladies did not mind the attention, deciding it was better to be a witch than a nobody. (And that's a fact!)

Anyway, witches would arrive at the Sabbath disguised as a black cat and riding a broomstick to function as the Devil's master of ceremonies. They would let out cat-like shrieks, which were called "howls from the Violin of Death"; and women who had "cats tied to their petticoats" would get wasted on wine and "dance with sorcerers" (the opposite of priests) crying "Har! Har! Sabbat! Sabbat!" just to piss off the Christians, who disapproved of partying on principle.

---

8. I made some of that up.

It is not known whether cats do in fact have a pact with the Devil, but according to *L'Evangile du Diable,* a Satanic bible which claims they do, the reason so few cats are seen during a Mardi Gras (which goes all the way back to the Middle Ages, in case you thought it was invented in New Orleans) is because the Evil One "invites them to feast with him"

Banished cat is home after 400-mile trek

MOSCOW (AP)—A year ago, Murka the cat was banished from her Moscow home for eating two canaries.

Today she is home, happy and pregnant, having found her way

cage in the apartment of her owner Vladimir Dontsov, the paper said.

A year later, Murka somehow unlocked the birdcage and killed the second.

"Thus it happened that the

On Oct. 19, Dontsov was on his way to work in Moscow when he spotted the cat on the fourth floor of their apartment building, dirty and hungry and minus part of her tail.

on that day. Also, cats "see everything, hear everything," and "Evil Spirits, warned just in time, always vanish, to disappear before we can see them."

The same book, *L'Evangile,* offers a nifty formula for making oneself invisible:

> Take 1 black cat, 1 new cooking pot, and 1 agate stone and cook them in water you have drawn from a fountain at midnight. Put the cat in the pot, hold the lid down with the left hand [presumably to keep the cat from rocketing out], let it boil for 24 hours and then, having placed the meat in a new dish, throw it over your shoulder and watch yourself till you no longer see yourself in a mirror.

If that doesn't work, I guess you try a new agate stone. Or a new cat.

Black cats were singled out as particularly evil in a papal bull (as in bullshit? Just joking) from Pope Gregory IX, in the 13th Century. That prejudice had long been festering, but Gregory now accused the heretical Cathars of breeding black cats to represent Evil and Shame. The same bull declared euthanasia and suicide to be evil and shameful and no substitute for martyrdom.

Murky as such reasoning may be, it likely is from

the Cathars' unholy breeding practices that we get the Church's pro-life doctrine, not to mention *Cat*holic and *cat*hedral and *cat*echism, and washed in the blood of the lamb.

Anyway, it was the English who invented the idea of a "familiar spirit," or a "familiar" or "imp," as a witch's animal assistant. This reckoned, for no good reason, that the Devil gave each witch a low-ranking demon in the form of a household animal to advise her and perform small malicious errands. Because cats were the most common household animal, they became the one most frequently regarded as a "familiar."

Kitten stomper fined $1,000

A man who stomped on his wife's kitten and fed it to his snarling pit **bull has been convicted of animal cruelty and fined nearly $1,000.**

But a California Superior Court judge refused a recommendation by the Probation Depart-

ment that Robert Graham spend 10 weekends in jail. Graham was given three years' probation in addition to the fine.

Graham's estranged wife Kathy told Bakersfield cops that he came to her home and argued with her.

He then grabbed her kitten out of her arms, threw it on the ground and jumped up and down on it before tossing it to his pit bull.

Mrs. Graham said the kitten was dead by the time she pried it away from the ferocious dog.

— *LAURI CORNELL* WEEKLY WORLD NEWS May 10, 1988

Such suspicions gained the cat considerable respect from strangers, but it also had its downside. Sometimes the mere possession of a cat was evidence of witchery, and both the alleged witch and her cat were burned, drowned, or tortured to death. This afforded both the opportunity to establish their innocence by failing

Pit bull dog's attack on poodle launches cat's career as a hero

to survive. Witch-hunters accepted these errors as God's way of harvesting souls, of improving the breed, or of narrowing the field, or something.

As mentioned earlier, some women readily confessed to being witches. In the Suffolk trials of 1645, Ann Usher's admissions were reported in a manner that the modern student of sexology might find instructional:

> She felt a thing like a small cat come over her legs once or twice. After that, she felt two things like butterflies in her

secret parts, with itchings, dancings, and sucking. And she felt them with her hands, and rubbed them, and killed them.

The fate of Ann Usher and her supernatural pussy are not recorded, but the feeling and rubbing sounds a little like masturbation, and the idea of demonic sucking seemed to excite witch-hunters no end. That concept was imported to America by the clergyman Cotton Mather whose preoccupation with "imps sucking persons" probably reflected some kind of sexual desire (the blow job?) and helped fuel the witchcraft hysteria in New England, which led to the Witch Trials of 1692.

ON THE BRIGHTER SIDE

As if its demonic associations did not cause the cat enough grief during the Middle Ages, the Gauls, before they took over France, were sacrificing cats instead of people to ward off bad luck. To the extent that cats replaced humans it represented social progress, though not, perhaps, from the cat's point of view. But even after the Gauls moved in the French still were hard on cats.

About 1320, at Metz, a town in the Moselle district, the bishop took pity on a condemned witch and contrived to have her freed under cover of smoke from an execution fire. He had a cat tossed into the flames to supply the proper sound effects, and when the probably-hairless cat also escaped, the

Lucky cat still has 8 lives left after his 14-story fall!

By DICK DONOVAN

Sky-diving Fluffy the cat burned up one of his nine lives when he plunged 14 stories from an apartment house balcony — and lived to purr about it!

The snow-white daredevil suffered relatively minor bruises and a few broken bones in one paw in his 140-foot

impressionable villagers decided they had seen the soul of the witch come bounding out. From that time on, cat-roasting became an annual ritual, employed as a kind of preventative medicine. This continued until

1773 when Mme. d'Armentieres, wife of the governor of Trois-Eveches, mercifully halted the practice.

On the brighter side, in the practice of *white* magic, the cat often became a desirable fetish, a talisman, an amulet, a lucky charm. Unfortunately, sometimes the lucky charm or amulet was walled up in a foundation to ensure the solidity of a building.

Much easier on the cat was the evoking of its other powers. The following formula comes from Mr. Hermes: "If you wish to see what others cannot see, rub your eyes with cat's dung and the fat from a white hen mixed together with wine."

Hermes does not indicate what others cannot see, but what *you* will see, if you follow his instructions, is cat shit.

Catlore permeates the Old World and the New and is, thankfully, less often involved with violence. Sometimes this takes the form of proverbs like "handsome cats and fat dung heaps are the sign of a good farmer." The European proverb that "a scalded cat dreads even cold water" has its Arab counterpart in "A cat bitten once by a snake dreads even rope." And virtually all cultures have some variation on several popular themes, including "when the cat's away, the mice will play," "all cats are gray in the dark," and "wherever mice laugh at the cat, there you will find a hole."

Pets Are Not Food in U.S., SPCA Will Advise Immigrants

By PENELOPE McMILLAN, *Times Staff Writer*

The Los Angeles Society for the Prevention of Cruelty to Animals is putting together an educational campaign to teach immigrants that American culture "does not tolerate the consumption of dogs and other domestic pets as food," according to Edward C. Cubrda, the group's executive director.

In the wake of a controversial court case this month involving two Cambodian refugees who ate a German shepherd puppy, Cubrda said his organization will try in particular to reach immigrants from countries such as Cambodia, Korea, Vietnam and the Philippines, where dogs are reputedly considered delicacies.

In those parts of France where cats weren't being tortured there existed a belief in a *matagot*, or magician-cat. This corresponded to the *chat d'argent* of Brittany, who could serve nine masters and make all of them rich. As it happens, this also was a black cat and had the power to attract wealth to an owner who loved it and fed it sumptuously. What you have to do is "lure the *matagot* with a plump chicken, grab him by the tail, put him in a sack, and surreptitiously take him home without once looking back." Which doesn't make any sense, but not much of this cat history does.

Anyhow, you are then required to put the above cat in a chest and share your food with him every time you eat, giving him the first mouthful. Do this a few times and you will find, beside him in the chest, a gold coin. Considering all the bad things that the French had been doing to cats, it's possible that this one is so relieved at not being burned or tortured or eaten that it laid gold coins to show its appreciation. (Some cat-fancier probably snuck this idea into his own cat history book and should be thanked for doing that. Especially by cats.)

The cat fared well enough in some parts of Brittany, where it was believed that the coat of every black cat includes one hair, and only one, that is perfectly white. This hair is reputed to be a powerful charm,

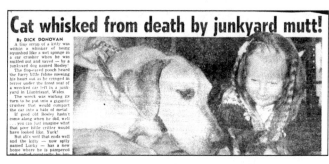

Cat whisked from death by junkyard mutt!

By DICK DONOVAN

A tiny scrap of a kitty was within a whisker of being squashed like a wet sponge in a car crusher when he was sniffed out and saved — by a junkyard dog named Booley!

The flop-eared pooch heard the furry little feline mewing his heart out as he cringed in terror under the front seat of a wrecked car left in a junkyard in Llantrisant, Wales.

The wreck was waiting its turn to be put into a gigantic crusher that would compact the car into a bale of metal.

If good old Booley hadn't come along when he did, well . . . you can just imagine what that poor little critter would have looked like. Yuck!

But all's well that ends well and the kitty — now aptly named Lucky — has a new home where he is pampered and petted constantly by her.

and the person who can find it and pluck it (without getting scratched?) can use it to become either lucky in love or very wealthy. Why this white hair cannot do both, or whether one excludes the other, is not explained, so you can only imagine the dilemma facing a fellow who is very horny and has found the hair but can't make up his mind.

Meanwhile, in the American Ozarks, a girl who is undecided about a marriage proposal may "Leave it to the cat." This requires plucking three hairs from a cat's tail, wrapping them in white paper, and putting them under her doorstep. After one week she checks to see if the hairs have arranged themselves into what looks like a Y or an N, for Yes or No (obviously), and she answers her suitor accordingly. (Quaint as this ritual sounds, I suspect its real purpose is to buy Miss Daisy Mae enough time to get the results of her pregnancy test.)

In many ages and many places cats have been associated with wifely infidelity. Folklore frequently describes the metamorphosis of women into cats for the purpose of sneaking out of the house at night, while their husbands sleep, to visit their lovers, in whose presence they transform back into women and get laid. The fact that husbands had no equivalent folklore and probably got out a lot, suggests this screwing-around technique was wishful thinking on the part of the ladies.

She gave all her food to her pets

Loving oldster dies — so her cats can live!

Cat loving spinster Joan Hall slowly starved herself to death so that her 100 pampered pets wouldn't go hungry.

"She neglected to feed herself so she could spend all her money on the cats," said neighbor Stephen Smith. "She really loved them. There was said Mrs. Dunsford. "She

On the other hand, male folklore, especially in the Orient, does recognize "benefactor cats" who are good luck in certain manly endeavors. Japanese sailors, for instance, believed that cats of three colors were able to predict storms, even if they couldn't do much about them. Also in Japan, the mythical boogeyman Neko-Bake was a cannibalistic sorcerer who allegedly took the shape of a cat in order to enter houses and "eat disobedient children."[9]

---

9. Among Doctor Naismith's many public services is his campaign to introduce the Neko-Bake idea into Western child-care literature as a replacement for Santa Claus, whose reward for good behavior is strictly seasonal.

THE CAT AND THE LAW

If cats caught hell during much of their history there was, at the same time, a certain amount of legal protection afforded the creatures when that suited a particular ruler or society.

It will be remembered, for instance, that during its heydays of divinity in Egypt cat-killing was punishable by death. But even the natural death of a cat required a period of mourning that included head-shaving, which even the most besotted cat-lover might today find objectionable.

If such cat-zeal has had a backlash in modern times, it may be that the protections cats enjoyed were the work of lawyers. St. Ives, the patron saint of lawyers, is commonly represented in the company of a cat, and that one famous cat fancier has observed that "the profound wisdom, the concealed claws, the stealthy approach and the final spring, all seem to typify the superior attorney."

> **Cat-shooting experiment draws fire from Congress**

In any case, Welsh laws concerning the rights of "domestic lions" were formulated in the 10th Century, and the canon law in 12th Century England forbade nuns, even abbesses, the wearing of skins costlier than those of lambs and cats. That may not sound like good news for cats, but it probably led to a 13th Century ruling that prohibited those same holy women from keeping any animal other than a cat. But it wasn't until 1818 that a decree was issued at Ypres, in Flanders, forbidding the throwing of cats from towers as part of that town's annual Christmas celebration. (I think it's in Spain where they still do that, and the pro-cat people raise a stink about it.)

In the Middle Ages, when animals could be tried for crimes, the defendants mainly were dogs, cows, oxen, and goats, with cats appearing as witnesses. Indeed,

HOW MY CAT CAME BACK FROM THE DEAD under Germanic law they also could be called as witnesses in the prosecution of human thieves and murderers. Those convicted rarely escaped the death penalty, but how a cat indicates guilt, or how you cross-examine a cat, I have no idea.

The monetary value of cats differed from place to place and time to time, but they were first given worth in South Wales. The value of a kitten from birth to the opening of its eyes was a penny (then equal to the value of a lamb, kid, goose, or hen). After that it was valued at twopence (equal to a cock or a gander) until it killed its first mouse, which made it worth fourpence (the same as a sheep or a goat).

The Dimetian and Gwentian Codes concerned themselves more with establishing the value of a cat in terms of wheat, specifying the animal to be worth whatever amount of the grain was required to cover it when "held by its tail over a clean, even floor." How they got a cat to hold still for such a stunt isn't known, but the same region's sense of humor was evident in a ruling that, in cases of divorce, the husband got the cat.

Welsh law once held that a community required "nine buildings, one herdsman, one plough, one kiln, one churn, one cock, one bull, and one cat" to qualify as a "lawful hamlet."[10]

The cat seems to have lent itself nicely to "lawyering" in other situations. In 1865, Monsieur Richard, the *juge de paix* (that's French for Justice of the Peace) of Fontainebleau, had to rule in a lawsuit against a citizen whose garden traps had caught fifteen of his neighbors'

---

10. Some ethologists believe this to be origin of the expression "cock and bull story."

cats. M. Richard's tedious decision ultimately favors the plaintiff:

> [T]hat all goods being either movables or immovables according to article 516 of the Code Napoleon, it results therefrom that the cat, contrary to article 128 of the same code, is incontestably a movable protected by the law, and therefore that the owners of the animals which are destroyed are entitled to claim the application of article 479, Clause I, of the Penal Code, which punishes those who have voluntarily caused damage to the movable property of others.

An even more Solomonic decision came down from the sheriff's court in Perth, Scotland, in the case of a cat that had slain a neighbor's pigeon on yet another neighbor's property:

> [I]t was quite legitimate for the plaintiff to keep a pigeon, but just as much so for the defendant to keep a cat. The plaintiff's plea is that the natural instinct of the feline race is to prey on birds as well as mice. So it was argued that the owner of the cat should prevent the possibility of its coming into contact with its favourite sport. But it is equally true that the owner of a bird should exercise similar precaution to prevent its coming within the range of a hostile race....

> In the present case it appears that both the quadruped and the winged animal were in trespass on neutral territory. It was the duty of the plaintiff to take the guardianship of the bird said to be so valuable and therefore both owners are equally to blame and the case must be

viewed as arising from natural law, for which neither owner without *culpa* can be answerable.

In the U. S. many cases involving cats have come before the courts, but none has so outraged cat owners as the decision from the attorney general of Maryland that a cat, owing the natural wildness of its nature, is *not* property and that stealing one, even an expensive Maltese, was not an indictable offense. In another case, however, the owner of a cat was held not liable for its killing of a neighbor's canary-bird on account of his pet's "predatory habits that are a remnant of its wild nature."

THE DEEP END

Except for their mouse-catching, efforts to impress cats into the service of mankind have generally met with failure. According to Doctor Naismith, travelers who became snow-bound in the Swiss alps learned (look out!) not to depend on the St. Bernard cats that had been bred for the strength and endurance needed in rescue work. Of course the Swiss, reluctant to concede mistakes, then tried importing Tibetan Sherpas to lead the rescue cats, from whose necks were suspended small casks of brandy.

When that arrangement also failed, the casks were hung around the necks of the Sherpas, who in their great furry outfits resembled large long-haired dogs. It was not until the middle of the 19th Century, Naismith says, that the Swiss discovered the wily Sherpas were replacing themselves with the dogs whose hair was similar in color.

Pet cat kills great-granny with just a single scratch

IN A TERRIBLE freak accident, a woman's pet black cat turned out to be the ultimate in

rival at a local hospital.
A post-mortem examination revealed the elderly woman had perished from shock caused by loss

Margaret Fortune-Hiseman, who says:
"I don't want Heidi blamed in any way The cat is a much-loved family

When this ruse was discovered (the ski lodges had

been filling up with free-spending Sherpas), the nimble-witted Swiss declared their breeding experiments to have developed the now-famous St. Bernard dog. The St. Bernard became glorified in legend and literature until 1961, when it was replaced by the motorized Sno-Cat, which the Swiss considered a vindication of their original rescue plan.

While I can't vouch for that story, or this one, Doctor Naismith insists that in the Deep South houndcats were used for tracking escaped slaves until the Confederacy was defeated in the Civil War. After 1864, Yankee Carpetbaggers subjugated the Southern Rednecks and freed all their sad-faced, flop-eared houndcats, ending that quaint ante-bellum tradition.

Doctor Naismith also claims that during World War I, attempts to train guard cats were abandoned during the Muse-Argonne Campaign. It seems the animals spent all their time licking mud off themselves, but they did prove useful in the rodding of cannon barrels. Soaked down with Hoppe's No. 9, a cat would be loaded into the breech of an artillery piece and the discomfort caused by the solvent would cause it to scramble the length of the barrel, removing the powder residue. White cats were particularly suited for this because the cleanness of a bore could be judged by the animal's color change. The first cat through the barrel typically emerged quite black, but when a white cat came out still white the gun

Cat fight shapes up over proposal to unleash law on footloose felines

By Kerry Luft

Elmhurst Ald. Guy Spinelli wants to treat cats like dogs.
He thinks the city should consider a law requiring cat owners to

Control, they get no help. That's because Elmhurst's current law says there's no such thing as a stray cat. "We don't have an ordinance against stray cats, so

munal space are so much smaller that an animal just cannot run free.
"We need to encourage con-finement to protect the

was ready to be put back in service.

During Prohibition, flappers in skimpy dresses would outfit their cats in cute little costumes with secret pockets for carrying hip-flasks (according to three newspaper articles), and this expression may must have evolved into the term "hip," as in smart, or smart-ass, or something. In the late 1960s the general public denigrated "hip" into "hippies," referring to the drug-addled flower children who turned on, tuned in, and dropped out, just to annoy their elders.

Let us conclude our history of cats with this excerpt from *Tiger in the House* (Knopf, 1920) by that all-time cat nut Carl Van Vecten:

> We have much to learn from the cat, we men who prefer to follow the slavish habits of the dog or the ox or the horse. If men and women would become more feline, indeed, I think it would prove the salvation of the human race. Certainly it would end war, for cats will not fight for an idea in the mass, having no faith in mass ideals, although a single cat will fight to the death for his own ideals, his freedom of speech and expression. The dog and the horse, on the other hand, perpetuate war, by group thinking, group acting, and serve further to encourage popular belief in that monstrous panacea, universal brotherhood.

If you think Van Vecten is losing it, remember that he's just written a 100,000-word book about cats. He babbles on:

> For the next war...man himself will become extinct. But the cat will survive.
>
> [The] great principles are obeyed by all cats to such an extent that twenty, a hundred, a thousand will willing give their lives, which they might easily save, to preserve an instinct, a racial memory, which will serve to perpetuate the feline race. The result will be that, after the cataclysm, out of the mounds of heaped-up earth, the piles and wrecks of half-buried cities, the desolated fields of

grain, and the tortured orchards, the cat will stalk, confident, self-reliant, capable, imperturbable, and philosophical. He will bridge the gap until man appears again and thcn he will sit on new hearths and again will teach his mighty lesson to ears and eyes that again are dumb and blind....

Which should be enough history of cats to choke one, as they say.

For falling cats, 7th story can be a lucky number

San Francisco Examiner

SAN FRANCISCO—The higher they are, the easier they fall, sometimes.

In what sounds like a joke from a Larson car...

after two days of observation in the [animal] hospital, having suffered nothing worse than a chipped tooth and mild pneumothorax," a type of lung injury, said physiologist Jared Diamond of the Medical School at University of C...

story reversal in death rates for cats?

Diamond said several factors, including mass and surface area, control how a falling creature hits the ...

"may relax and extend the limbs more horizontally in flying-squirrel fashion."

This would succeed in "not only reducing the velocity of fall but also ...

From venerated to reviled and back again, history's cat obviously is a tough old bird and not one that's chicken-livered, or an old dog to whom you can't teach new tricks. It didn't survive by being as stupid as it would lead us to believe, which may be the secret of its success. Peasants can be exploited but only intellectuals are persecuted, so it is a testament to the cat's foxiness that it plays 'possum until it is has wormed its way into our hearts. And after that medley of metaphors we need to get:

BACK TO BUSINESS

Where were we? Psycatherapy. Owner Guilt. Tough Love. History. So let's stop pussy-footing around and consider where our cat is coming from, where it's going, and how it's going to get there.

At the outset we should ask, *Can your cat walk and chew gum at the same time?*

Probably your cat doesn't want to. Probably it is basking in lassitude, on your bed or in your easy-chair, thinking, *If that son of a bitch wants me to move, he's going to have to get his fat ass over here and pick me up or shoo me away with something. Then I'll give him my abused look and walk off in a huff. After that I'll pout. And when he leaves, I'll go back and claw things. Hmmm. I don't like the looks of that book he's reading.*

Which leads our Doctor Naismith to observe:

> A look of consternation tells us that our exercises are working. A Marine Corps drill sergeant is hard on his boys only because he loves them. He wants to tune their minds, build their bodies, hone their wits, turn them into highly-skilled and bloodthirsty killing machines. To see the fruits of his labor are his reward.
>
> With a cat we must settle for less, but its strut and swagger will depend on how well it develops some of those same qualities. We want to be able to say:

NO PAIN, NO GAIN

The fact is, our cat has a lot of untapped potential that can be brought out by an understanding owner—an owner who understands that his cat has fooled him into thinking it's a finished product. Well, so are diamonds before they are cut. And fish before they are fried.

TALKING CAT!

Amazing kitty says more than 100 words, say experts

The secret, then, is to *not* try to teach your cat. Instead, the owner can prevail by violating pussy-cat's expectations, by deliberately sending out mixed messages (a practice not unknown in human relationships), and by catching it by surprise.

For instance, the owner can fire up the electric can-opener without having a can, or open the refrigerator door only to close it again, or fill the cat's food bowl with cornflakes. And the litter-box that normally

A Brief History of Cats 27

resides in one corner of the bathroom can one day appear in the other corner, then in the hallway, or wherever. These variations on old themes will deny your cat the sense of security that comes with predictability.

And a cat confounded is a cat wide awake, a cat that is seeking order where there is no order. A cat which, in the absence of routines, becomes befuddled and resorts to the playfulness and cuteness that made it so lovable in the first place.

The objective here is not to break our cat's spirit. Insofar as the cat thinks it already has reached perfection, only by taking it down a notch or two will we help it see things in proper perspective.

In short, only by showing the cat who is boss will we develop in it the *owner-respect* that is either genetically absent or has been bred out of it through generations of pampering. We show it who is boss by engineering a humbling experience that opens pussy's mind to the possibility it is not, in fact, the ultimate, final, and highest product of animal evolution. To that end we want a cat who knows it's been hired but is *still on probation.*

So the free ride is over. It's time to get to work.

THE PUSS 'N BOOT CAMP

GETTING YOUR CAT IN FIGHTING TRIM

Getting your cat in fighting trim will not be easy, especially if it is an Apartment Cat whose greatest challenge is getting you to feed it. If it is a House Cat, one that goes outside, it is bound to encounter other cats, streetwise cats, and you don't want your gray or black or orange cat turning into a yellow cat. It would be galling to think that the caterwauling of some feral feline could freak your cat out, vanquish it from the field of honor, and send it racing home to the safety of its hearth. This would be humiliating for the cat and result in a self-loathing, anxiety-ridden, stressed-out cat, mired in depression.

Not healthy, in other words.

Of course, you don't want your kitty to go out and pick fights, or to put itself in harm's way by challenging somebody's pit-bull. But the very fact that your cat can take care of itself in a combat situation—and knows it—will cause it to exude self-confidence and discourage any bullying by other cats. The best defense is a good offense. In other words,

WALK SOFTLY BUT CARRY A BIG STICK

So how does one's cat develop the proper swagger that will make the both of you proud?

Training!

Which doesn't mean you can take some elderly, sedentary, overweight bozo of a cat and whip it into shape. It *does* mean you can start with an ignorant and inexperienced youth of a cat, just like the Army does, and through the judicious use of hardship and discomfort raise its threshold of fear. As any successful brawler will tell you, the fellow who isn't afraid of getting hurt is the one who wins the fight. Unless the other fellow has a gun, maybe.[11]

Russkies make nice hats out of stray cats

Stray cats have a tough life in commie Russia where they are poisoned if they are caught or even worse

Anyway, your cat's fear can be reduced homeopathically by giving it little doses of discomfort—doses that gradually immunize it from the fear of getting hurt.

The quickest way to do this is to have your little kitty play with a little kid. The tyke will pull kitty's tail, carry it upside down, follow it under the bed, things like that. Having no frame of reference, kitty will grow up thinking this sort of thing is normal, just *the way things are.*

It is the grown-up cat who will have to reconsider its situation in light of our Puss 'n Boot training program.

LIGHTING A FIRE UNDER YOUR CAT

This is a figure of speech. No rational, reasonable, sensible, loving cat owner would light an actual fire under his or her cat. However, it is not necessary for his or her cat to be certain of this.

One of the spices in life is to number among your friends at least one who is charming, witty, interesting, and therefore fun to know, but who is not entirely sensible, does not always exercise good judgment, and who thereby entertains his friends by doing things that are *really stupid.*

---

11. Remember the old joke about the guy who brings a knife to a gunfight?

Lighting fires under animals should not be one of these things. But if your cat (who probably does not understand "figure of speech") has reason to think that its owner has even entertained such a thought, you become, in its estimation, a far more interesting person, one whose mild manner, generosity, and pleasant disposition might in fact be overcompensation for *terrible sadistic impulses* that he must constantly control.

MOONING

One of a cat's less endearing qualities is its practice of mooning.

If you are sitting at the table, trying to read something, your cat may walk by with its tail held high and provide a proctologist's view of its poop-hole.

I had to make that poetic because it's so disgusting. Of course your cat may only be harking back to its kittenhood, when mama cat would lick its little bum to relax its little sphincter so kitty could make do-do.

Which is also pretty disgusting. But once it grows up the cat is telling you, *Kiss my ass.*

Whether your cat is black or white or orange, most veterinarians advise against spraying its puckered part a matching color. Instead, if you are a girl cat owner, use a quick burst of hair spray. If you are a boy cat owner, one squirt of WD-40 should do the trick.

IMPRESSING YOUR CAT

Its ability to ignore its master is what give our cat

its stubbornness, its sense of independence, its attitude. These tell its owner to not expect much of it. They simplify the cat's life and it may be judged intelligent simply because, when it craps, it covers it up.

Big deal. In carnival sideshows there are chickens who can beat human beings at tic-tac-toe. So if we want our cat's attention, we need to worry it a little, using one of the following Arousal techniques.

Technique No. 1: Get down on all fours and bark like a dog.

Technique No. 2: Sprinkle catnip on the floor and roll around in it, purring and looking enraptured and utterly witless—like you are a cat.

These actions will make your cat think you are nuts, and since nuts are unpredictable, sometimes dangerous, your pet will start keeping an eye on you.

MOTIVATING YOUR CAT

Once a cat has progressed beyond kittenhood and adolescence, all its pleasures are passive. Only an *alert* cat, a cat that is *stimulated,* a cat whose ennui has been dispelled by the *thrill of a kill* will benefit from our visit to a sporting goods store, where we will find the noise-making devices invented for the hunting community.

Even a comatose cat leaves someone on duty in its neurotransmitter room. Its natural born aptitudes may have been mitigated by the bowls of food that are faithfully served by its slothful owner, but that same slothful owner can use these noise-making devices to sound like an animal in distress. Or who is horny. Or both.

One device is the kind you blow into and it makes quacking or chirping sounds. Another involves sticks and boxes made from certain woods that are scraped or twanged to produce the squawks and squeals of an Old Crow or a Wild Turkey.

Your cat may get off on any of these. Its mental watch captain will bolt upright and activate a psychic klaxon that goes

Ahhh-OOOOH-gah!
Ahhh-OOOOH-gah!

in the cat's Combat Information Center, signaling *"Battle Stations! Battle Stations!"* and bringing your cat to RED ALERT. Kitty's head will jerk up, eyes wide, ears scanning like radar antennae to get a fix on the noise.

Either that, or the ears will go flat, the cat will look petrified, and it will dart to the nearest hiding place.

Meaning you can think of your pet not as a cat but a chicken.

EARNING YOUR CAT'S CONFIDENCE

Having made your cat alert and having gotten its attention, we now must gain its trust by lowering its fight or flight response. We'll do this through a program of what I'll call Systematic Desensitization. Which I've decided will make it brimful of self-confidence. Skimping on this could leave us with a neurotic cat, a mentally unbalanced cat, a cat that will not fully benefit from the exercises in this manual.

Just before feeding time, pick kitty up, hold it upside down, and start raising and lowering it. At first the cat's adrenal gland will activate the internal gyroscope that makes it land on its feet.[12] But since it isn't being tossed, it will sooner or later (my Floozy took four days) decide the situation is temporary and stop trying to invert. It will also decide you get off on this, and if it's going to get fed it might as well accept it as some weird kind of pre-mealtime foreplay.

DOES CURIOSITY KILL THE CAT?

We all have heard that "Curiosity Killed the Cat." However, looking inside an empty paper sack is not mere curiosity, it is how a cat establishes that nothing dangerous is hiding in there. And if it goes inside the sack, peeking out, it is only exercising its predatory instincts—Skulking With Intent to Lurk.

Neither of these is a punishable offense, and if we want to judge the effectiveness of our Puss 'n Boot program we

Stranded cat lands his owner in big trouble with the law!

When Spooky the cat got stuck in a tree, James Otts went up after him — and got stuck right alongside the scared kitty.

Before the day was over, Otts had been rescued from the tree — but was stuck in the arms of the law.

The uproar began when Spooky got marooned in a 100-foot tree in Smyrna, Ga., and the Fire Department refused to go up after him.

Otts, 25, was so disgusted

the scene — and before long they hauled him downtown.

The would-be rescuer was held at police headquarters

can set out a paper sack and place in it one of those little round face mirrors.

If your cat hunches and bristles and goes *grrrrowwwww*, your cat has earned its stripes.

---

12. According to the *Guinness Book of World Records*, a cat can be dropped from a pretty good height (I forget just what) and it won't go *splat*.

If, however, your cat freaks out, we must ask ourselves, will our Puss 'n Boot Camp increase its playfulness and restore its entertainment value? Or will our Puss 'n Boot Camp only provide the counseling needed by our kitty-cat's *owner*?

Either way, this manual will have served its purpose. So this Puss 'n Boot Camp should not be a license to bully or abuse your cat. To develop its mental muscles, yes. To test its coping abilities, yes. To make it a little uncomfortable, maybe. *But only for its own good.*

FEEDING YOUR CAT

"Finicky" is the word often used to describe a cat and its food and the way it ignores you until it decides to eat. The author remembers reading, in the *Smithsonian* or *National Geographic* or someplace, that lions and tigers and so forth hunt individually rather than in packs. This means they eat when they are hungry and not because the pack made a kill for a sit-down meal. Which is why our cute little cat waits until its hunger curve has intersected its laziness curve and it gets up off its butt. While a kitten can be raised on Dry

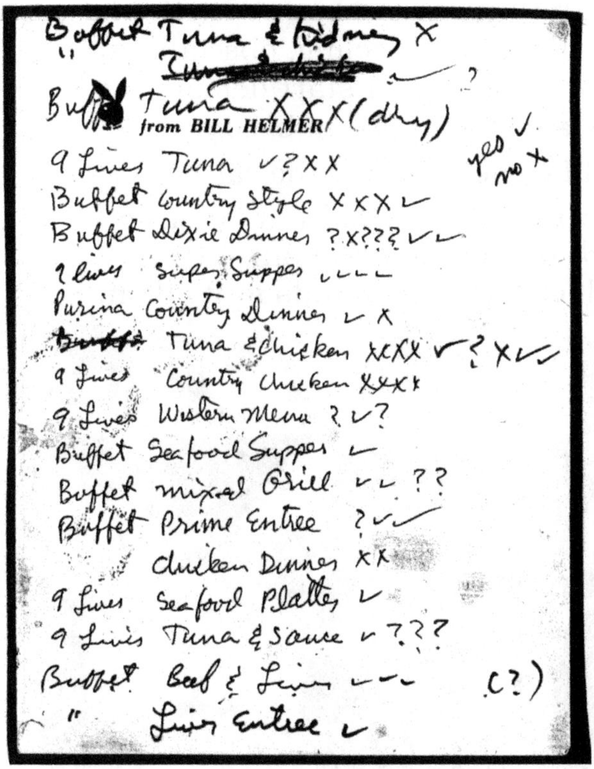

[Handwritten note, headed "from BILL HELMER":]

Buffet Tuna & Kidney X
~~Tuna & Kidney~~ ?
Buffet Tuna XXX (dry)   yes ✓ / no X
9 Lives Tuna ✓? XX
Buffet Country Style XXX ✓
Buffet Dixie Dinner ? X??? ✓✓
9 Lives Super Supper ✓✓✓✓
Purina Country Dinner ✓ X
~~Buffet~~ Tuna & Chicken XXX ✓ ? X✓✓
9 Lives "Country Chicken XXX ✗
9 Lives Western Menu ? ✓?
Buffet Seafood Supper ✓
Buffet mixed Grill ✓✓ ??
Buffet Prime Entree ? ✓
" Chicken Dinner XX
9 Lives Seafood Platter ✓
9 Lives Tuna & Sauce ✓ ?,??
Buffet Beef & Liver ✓✓✓   (?)
"   " Liver Entree ✓

cat food (if it doesn't know there is such a thing as Wet), the Established Cat will use food and feeding to manipulate the owner who believes that he or she can alternate between Wet and Dry, and get away with it.

Offered Dry, our grown cat will look up with an expression of contempt as if to say, *You can stick that crap where the sun don't shine.* Even if its little tummy is craving nourishment, it will not succumb to Dry so long as you are in the same room, watching. If you go out of the room your cat may nibble a little just to keep from starving, but not until you come through with Wet will it engage in actual eating.

And after that it will soon want those little cans of gourmet cat food that cost twice as much as Gerber's. Then, when your cute little kitty has reduced its anxious owner to a sniveling, driveling, obsequious, pussy-pampering neurotic, it will start demanding the cat equivalent of a filet wrapped in bacon.

Which is not good for the owner or the cat.

We could end up with One Fat Cat, but fat or not, this problem cannot be handled like our kitty is a dog. A dog will gobble anything it finds in its dish, or that comes from the table, or it finds on the floor, or doesn't gobble back. Your cat's Wet Food addiction is not so easily cured, however, until you start *making mistakes.* So feed it dog food, which is wet and comes

from a can but doesn't taste good. Once your cat decides you are a real screw-up, switch back and forth from the Wet dog food to cat food that is Dry.

If the food switching takes too long, throw a stick and say "Fetch." Or give your cat a bone.

REFUSES TO SLEEP ON ITS PALLET

Once your cat determines the places it must not sleep, it will sleep only in those places, ignoring the fancy pallet that cost good money at the local Walmart. The result will be cat hair on the couch, or your favorite easy-chair, or on anything made of fabric. (Dark fabrics are less of a problem if your cat is black.)

Or our kitty may find sleeping places that are secret, just to make its owner worry. *Where's the cat? Has anybody seen the cat?* Which gets one to looking in closets and under beds, wondering why the cat is *not* on the couch, the easy-chair, etc.

One can obviate this problem by buying mousetraps. Get the classic spring-loaded kind, place them in various cat resting places and watch what happens.

That, or the cat spots the traps, gets excited, and starts looking for a mouse.

HOUSE RULES

The easiest way to exhibit strength of character is to post notices that substitutes for strength of character—forbidding one thing or mandating another. Such notices can be posted on the wall next to the cat's food bowl or litter-box as Rules of the Establishment.

Rules of the Establishment won't mean anything to the cat, but its owner will find it easier to say No (as the cat tries to look like an African famine victim) and shake your head, shrug helplessly, and point at an official notice that says

NO FOOD BEFORE 5 PM
—The Management

This is a practice known the world over to bureaucrats, supervisors, and middle-management toadies. Not only do humans derive a sense of power by instituting rules, but they can cite them as their excuse for behaving churlishly, refusing to make exceptions, and otherwise avoiding the use of their brains, common sense, or good judgment.

This cheap trick (one that falls somewhere between "My hands are tied" and "I'm only following orders") helps weak pet owners stand firm in the face of appeals to one's generosity, which cats are unethical enough to exploit at every opportunity.

ERASING YOUR CAT

At the risk of disillusioning millions of cat owners, we must advise that our pet's practice of rubbing against furniture or one's leg is not a display of affection. It is territorial acquisition—staking out property claims.

Everything a cat brushes against picks up its scent, and not until a cat has spread its scent the length and breadth of its domain does it relax and become boring.

This is not fair to the cat. Its life loses

Cat gets credit card but his owner can't

ONLY IN AMERICA can anyone be given the opportunity to seek financial reward and happiness, regardless of race, creed or species.

In fact, cat owner Janet Ringgenburg found out *by KATHY HART* some Americans are more equal than others. She can't get credit anywhere, but her black-and-white tomcat doesn't have any problems proving his credibility.

When Janet got a letter from MasterCard/VISA, she thought her troubles were over — until she discovered the $5,000-limit credit card was reserved in "Fred's" name.

Joke

"When I got the notice in my mail, I thought it was a joke," Janet recalls. "They deny me a credit

its about a year ago to get coupons for the food that they regularly purchase.

No complaints

Some firm must have picked up Eustace's name from the form, and a computer spat it out on the letter for the credit card offer.

Fred hasn't complained about the family's calling attention to the error, even though he would have received his own card.

But Janet says she is thinking of sending in Fred's card application

How to Outsmart Your Cat

meaning when it has no new worlds to conquer, so when the odor does wear off Mr. Pussy will go back to work, marking things.

Our cat is not putting much thought into this, and it probably won't realize what is happening if its owner goes around laying hands on things—table legs, doorways, window sills—anywhere that erases the cat's scent and replaces it with his own.

This really puts a cat's nose out of joint. If you have friends who have cats, ask them to rub their own pussy down and use that piece

Top Russian scientists confirm:

AMAZING CAT TALKS!

By JOE BERGER
A cantankerous kitty
named General Don.

of cloth to erase your cat's territorial claims. Kitty will start checking the entire residence in search of a ghost cat. Or, better yet, a ghost *dog*.

LITTER-BOX REJECTION

If one's cat, for no apparent reason, starts peeing outside its litter-box, it means one of three things

1. *You should empty the litter-box.*
2. *Your cat has hemorrhoids.*
3. *Your Cat has an attitude.*

For No. 1, do what you have to do. For No. 2, also do what you have to do. But If it's No. 3, don a white coat, hang a stethoscope around your neck, and go *"HERE, kitty kitty. HERE, kitty kitty."*

WHEN CATS PLAY DUMB

In some situations, when your cat appears even less scrutable than usual, its owner may suspect that it's not inscrutable at all but merely being contrary.

For instance: if your cat meows to come in but when

you open the door it just sits there; or if it meows to go out and then won't go out. This is not contrariness. This is your cat being *passive-aggressive*, a subtle means by which it can express hostility without risk of retribution

Even if you did nothing to justify your cat's hostility, you may not have done enough to avoid it.

- You came in late for you-know-who's suppertime;

- Your choice of cat food has failed to please;

- You scolded your cat for barfing a hairball on the carpet.

Whichever the case, the obtuseness of Mr. Pussy may be that of the bureaucrat whose only job satisfaction comes from making people wait. This form of self-assertion is a variation on the sit-down strike, and the only way to deal with it is patience. Your patience. *A maddening amount of patience.*

- Kittycat does not wish to come in? Fine. Kitty can stay out.

- Kittycat does not wish to go out? Fine. Kitty can stay in.

- Kittycat does not care for its food? Fine. Maybe tomorrow kitty will be less choosy.

In short, one fights Dumb with Dumb. The passive-aggressive tactic doesn't work on people who are too stupid to perceive what's going on, so you remain

Attack of the Killer Cats

A study shows that those lovable furry pets decimate wildlife

W hile fond of his cat, British biologist Peter Churcher looked askance at its practice of dragging small mammals | bags and identifying the remains. If the cat had consumed the entire catch, the victim was simply recorded as an "unpleasantly persistent until your adversary, unable to wear you down, gives up.

SEX AND THE SINGLE CAT

Men more than women—*real* men, that is, not pansies who compensate for their sexual inadequacy by owning dogs—are sometimes conflicted about having their pussycat . . . ah . . . *fixed.*

Especially if it's a male cat.

It is not that real men dispute the benefits of having a cat that does not wander around, howling mournfully, spraying anywhere, or trying to hump one's teddy-bear. And it is not that real men don't sometimes envy the fellow whose lack of sex drive spares him the horniness that might otherwise get him in trouble. Rather, it is simply that real men can too easily imagine some jerk in a white labcoat picking up a scalpel and going for their private parts.

We're talking here about the kind of sentence that Southern judges like to lay on sex offenders.

We're talking about what lynch mobs do to other sexual miscreants.

We're talking major terrifying surgery.

We're talking about *CASTRATION!*[13]

---

13. Girl cat owners are indifferent if not downright callous about castration. Either they have no sensibilities in this area or they subconsciously want to emasculate all men. If you go to the zoo you'll see the boy animals chasing the girl animals all over the place, because the girl animals won't put out.

The fact that the author is unvasectomized has nothing to do with his views on sexual intercourse. No less an authority than the great child psychologist Bruno Bettelheim might well have advised against the neutering of pets in homes with male children whose œdipal conflicts might possibly be exacerbated by an inborn fear of that.

If there are no male children to consider, and if the cat doesn't know what's going to happen, and if it doesn't feel anything because of anesthesia, it won't know what it is missing—*e.g.*, loneliness, heartache, and despair.

Which leaves us with the question each cat owner must answer for himself:

IS IT BETTER TO HAVE LOVED AND LOST, OR NEVER TO HAVE LOVED AT ALL?

I don't think I got that right.

DOES YOUR CAT GET LONESOME?

Whether or not a single cat feels lonely when its owner is at work, or when its owner can't find his or her way home, is a matter of debate.

One school of thought holds that cats need companionship and attention so that they have something to ignore. Another school believes that so long as the food bowl is full and the litterbox gets emptied, the cat couldn't care less.

Doctors Assail Project in Which Cats Are Shot

From Associated Press

NEW ORLEANS—A Defense Department research program in which cats are shot in the head to

The first school is anthropomorphic in that it attributes human attitudes to an animal. The second is valid if the human is congenitally lazy, self-centered, and indifferent to everything except sleep, food, and sex.

Only humans confuse loneliness and horniness.

The notion that a single cat needs companionship stems from the belief that single children need brothers and sisters. This misinterprets the biological instinct to breed, to produce more offspring, only a few of whom will amount to anything and look after their parents in old age.

Social Security has taken care of that, as children nowadays are more likely to be parasites. And since a cat's owner is all the Social Security it needs, having two cats probably reflects the needs of the owner more than of the cat.

IS YOUR KITTY HAPPY?

Cats have few facial muscles with which to express emotions. Except for the ears, which may flatten, or the eyes, which may widen, there is little difference in gross[14] appearance between a cat that is happy and a cat that is sad. If you think your cat can glower, appear annoyed, look contemptuous, or show disgust, that's your imagination working.

But let's accept those possibilities and work at fostering expressions that look *perturbed* and *weirded out.*

Like good shepherd, nun worries about fate of her flock of cats

The Lord works in mysterious ways, and Sister Marijon Binder believes that cats are one of them. "They can teach us a lot about how to live with each other," she said. "I've learned so much from the cats—gentleness, loyalty, how to take care of others. I think I could write the gospel according

About the town

Barbara Brotman

Not that one would deliberately distress one's pussycat for the sake of amusement, but that could happen unintentionally. If, for instance, you came home carrying the mounted boar's head you

---

14. The author is advised that most people think the word gross means yukky instead of immediately obvious, as it is properly used here. Keep reading and maybe you'll learn something.

The Puss 'n Boot Camp

bought on eBay, your cat would have kittens, as they say. Only if you possess a streak of orneriness would you even think about something so hilarious, and only with a Smartphone would you take a picture of your cat at full Battle Stations, when it looks like an exploding hair grenade.

Just saying.

DOES YOUR CAT WITHHOLD AFFECTION?

Dogs wear their hearts on their sleeves—except for homicidal pit-bulls and the little *yap-yaps* that should be duct-taped to a stick and used for dusting. Fido is easy to read: he smiles, he laughs, he wags his tail. He growls, he whines, he hangs his head if he's done something naughty. Only a dog can look dog-tired.

Not so our cat, who gets a lot of mileage out of being inscrutable.

This inscrutability may give the impression of sagacity, intelligence, thoughtfulness, sapience, and judiciousness. The cat appears to be thinking and observing and one is reluctant to interrupt.

In fact, this is merely a labor saving device.

A cat's inscrutability is the mode in which it normally operates, and any departure from that routine is an exciting event for its owner: *Look, the cat is curious! Oh boy, the cat is playful! Ah, the cat is pissed!* And when the cat seems to display affection but isn't just angling for food, its delighted owner responds as though to a lover's wink.

Cool cats, chilly dogs

A freeze-dried pet is a friend forever

By Ron Laytner

PINELLAS PARK, Fla.— Sweetie sleeps with her eyes wide open in the cool darkness of suburban St. Petersburg in central Florida.

Sweetie isn't cold. The beloved pet rests on her own pillow bed, a soft

Cats have this advantage because they don't mind being ignored. Indeed, they often wish to be ignored, lest the attentions of kitty's owner cuts into its sleep. If a simple meow doesn't yield a bowl of food, climbing onto the owner's book, or newspaper, or chest, or face, is a guaranteed attention-getter. Or if the owner is comatose, sleeping one off in a real stupor, pussy will knead one's flesh with a hint of claw, or with more than a hint, till old Gulliver comes out of it.

When sated with love and able to get attention whenever needed, the cat accepts affection as its birthright and incurs no sense of obligation to an owner who, poor fool, only wanted some attention himself. Which leaves us with a case of

HAVES VS THE HAVE-NOTS

One can withhold affection till one turns blue in the face and get no rise out of kitty-cat. But if you

'LONELY' MAN KILLS 22 CATS!

A computer program analyst admitted that he strangled a kitten because he thought it was reject- | he was arrested after dumping a bag containing a dead cat into a garbage bin. According to defense attorney Rick Brooks, Farkas' | although Farkas blamed himself for the kitten's death, he immediately went out and adopted another one. But the second kitten wasn't | tor Mac Lindsay. Most of the cats Farkas killed were stolen, but some were acquired from animal shelters or through newspaper ads placed by peo-

acquire one of those Robot Cats[15] you can lavish affection on it,[16] and give it a pretty name (like Sweetikins), and turn it on so it does things, and talk to it, and stroke it in front of your increasingly curious cat. You can even do the mealtime cat-call that gets your pussy trotting to its food bowl, so you can say, *"Not you, Asshole."*[17]

Your cat may still sleep much of the time, but will dream that it has competition and lacks its owner's full attention.[18]

---

15. You know, the kind that's supposed to give old folks companionship.

16. Especially if you've rubbed somebody else's cat all over it.

17. Getting your cat jealous is easier when you have a real flesh-and-blood Guest Cat, but then you've got two cats to deal with.

18. Don't forget to put your Robot Cat away. You don't want your kitty to wait till you're gone and sniff it.

CAT BARF

The wise cat owner does not own a white carpet, which shows every hairball stain. Nor a black carpet, which shows every hair.[19] When he goes carpet-shopping, he buys something in the beige to light brown range that matches his cat's barf.

Pet experts recommend several ways to minimize the hairball problem. None of them work. Some sort of work, but have the downside of causing the cat to barf stuff much more staining than a nice firm hairball that looks like a turd and bums out overnight guests when they step on it. What bums them out even more is for the owner to pick it up, toss it in the toilet, then wipe his hands on his pants.[20]

Pets Are Not Food in U.S., SPCA Will Advise Immigrants

By PENELOPE McMILLAN, *Times Staff Writer*

The Los Angeles Society for the Prevention of Cruelty to Animals is putting together an educational campaign to teach immigrants that American culture "does not tolerate the consumption of dogs and other domestic pets as food," according to Edward C. Cubrda, the group's executive director.

In the wake of a controversial court case this month involving two Cambodian refugees who ate a German shepherd puppy, Cubrda said his organization will try in particular to reach immigrants from countries such as Cambodia, Korea, Vietnam and the Philippines, where dogs are reputedly considered delicacies.

The shade of carpet color should be tailored to the color of the hairball and depends on the brand of catfood. At the risk of being rewarded with a lifetime supply sent to me by its manufacturer, I recommend dry Friskies, especially Ocean Flavor.[21] The Friskies people have the morals of a drug dealer, however. Sacks of Friskies always contain coupons for sample cans of FancyFeast wet gourmet, which is like supplying crack to high school students.[22]

---

19. Unless, of course, your cat is black.

20. But this is a good way to get rid of a guest the next morning. See also Coyote Ugly. If Coyote Ugly isn't in this manual, it is because it's an affront to women and has been censored by a female editor who finds the joke offensive, because it deals with chewing off one's arm rather wake up the lady with whom one spent the night.

21. Ocean Flavor usually comes up semi-solid and color-fast, and if you let it set until it dries you can lift it off the carpet in one chunk.

22. Which probably blows my chance of any getting free Friskies.

EMBARRASSMENT EXERCISES

As with any toddler, man or beast, one of the most endearing qualities of a kitten is its awkwardness:

• *When it is so wrapped up in play that it tumbles off of something.*

• *When it tries so comically to emulate a lion stalking prey.*

• *When its leap is but a funny little hop.*

• *When it prances around, trying to bat some object into mouse-like life.*

Such cuteness is what makes it irresistible to anyone who forgets that our kitten will one day be a cat. And once a cat, its chief contribution to our pleasure

Dogs vs. Cats: Who's Really No. 1?

A recent survey shows that 34.7 million households in the U.S. have 52.4 million dogs; 27.7 million households have a total of 54.6 million cats, and 5.2 million households have 12.9 million pet birds.

The fascinating survey was conducted by the American

will be those brief moments of alertness at the sound of the fridge door or when answering the siren song of an electric can-opener.

Piss on that!

Apart from such events, the only time an adult cat is halfways interesting is when it has become self-aware and self-conscious because it is *screwing up*.

For reasons unknown to animal psychologists, the cat is capable of experiencing embarrassment, and because of this any clumsiness will cause it to *lose face*. How it behaves in an effort to *save* face is a hoot.

Consider the three things that a suave, poised, arrogant, oh-so-cool cat fears most—namely, Pratfalls, Leap Deprivation, and Shaving the Hair Off Your Cat.

1. PRATFALLS

Observe the cat as it runs somewhere, perhaps in response to the sound of an electric can-opener. Then observe the cat when it slips on a polished floor.

In itself this is no big deal; what's amusing is to watch the cat try to recover its dignity by assuming a sitting position and licking itself, as though that was its intention all along.

Stranded cat lands his owner in big trouble with the law!

When Spooky the cat got stuck in a tree, James Otts went up after him — and got stuck right alongside the scared kitty.

Before the day was over, Otts had been rescued from the tree — but was stuck in the arms of the law.

The uproar began when Spooky got marooned in a 100-foot tree in Smyrna, Ga., and the Fire Department refused to go up after him. Otts, 25, was so disgusted

the scene — and before long they hauled him downtown. The would-be rescuer was held at police headquarters

Causing this to happen deliberately not only provides a few chuckles but affords an owner the sense of superiority he will need when dealing with cats in their curmudgeonly mode. All one needs to do is wax the floor where the cat makes high-speed turns, and when the cat comes to grief, start laughing.

2. LEAP DEPRIVATION

Cats take inordinate pride in their ability to leap softly and silently to window sills and other surfaces from which they can peer outside or on which they can go to sleep. That pride is misplaced. Leaping ability was a gift of nature for the purpose of moving noiselessly in the wild. It is a gift that the cat has forgotten in this day of the pampered pussy. We should not denigrate this genetically preserved ability, but we can do something about the inordinate pride your cat takes in it.

Begin by noting the different locations—dresser top, window sill, *etc.*—to which the cat leaps for the purpose of napping or gazing out the window (probably to admire the birds or oversee its domain). Then, when the cat is not looking, put a handful of marbles or bottle caps or other small items on the spot where the leaping cat lands. And watch.

Sooner or later Mr. Cat will saunter over to its launching pad, execute its leap, and too late discover that its landing field is littered with such objects. The look of surprise is well worth capturing with your Smartphone that takes movies. And get the cat's look of chagrin when its touchdown sends the marbles or bottle caps flying.

It is a look that says *Oh Shit!,* but it should not be conducted so often that your pet gets the feline version of jet lag.

3. SHAVING THE HAIR OFF YOUR CAT

This would be a major humiliation and counter-productive, for a cat's appearance is important to maintaining the motivation it needs to become a *better* cat.

However, shaving the hair off somebody *else's* cat (okay, maybe one of those hairless cats, whatever) and posting a picture of it near your own cat's water bowl, can diminish the excessive licking it does when ignoring your *HERE, kitty-kitty, HERE, kitty-kitty.*

GETTING YOUR CAT'S GOAT

Peevishness ill becomes a cat whose owner has devoted so much love and effort to making its life comfortable. But peevishness is the attitude that often rewards the owner when Mr. Cat has developed a mannerism that becomes a habit and turns into a trait. At this point it is only fair that we give our cat something to be peevish *about.*

One sure way to peeve a cat is to put a book or the TV remote on its favorite sleeping place. Not something big enough to obstruct its sleep entirely, causing it to go sleep somewhere else, but something that the cat will decide *what comes will go* if it just waits long enough. And rather than surrender its private property, it will curl up around the object and *try* to sleep. But it won't be very *comfortable*.

Dog-eating divides West Coast

New York Times News Service

SAN FRANCISCO—Few issues so profoundly divide the multifarious cultural and religious groups that have multiplied on the West Coast in recent years as the relative gastronomic merits of the world's fauna.

The diner who relishes escargot in a French restaurant may turn

At which point you start adding more and more clutter until the cat realizes that you are trying to get its goat. Then you keep adding stuff till the cows come home, and it will think, *screw you.*

What we are doing here is borrowing a trick from the martial arts—using your opponent's strength against him.

For the cat will double-down, and not until you come up with something the size of a computer keyboard will it concede defeat. Then it will stomp off in snit, tail raised, its way of giving you the finger.

WHEN CATS POUT

Peevishness is one thing, and once the cat's goat has been gotten, and it knows it (this is your Prank), the usual response is to Pout. We can express the sequence graphically as follows:

PEEVISH → PRANK → POUT

In other words, Pout is what the cat does when its peevishness leads to your Prank and it feels Bested.

How to Outsmart Your Cat

What does the cat do when it is Bested? It Pees where it's not supposed to, as represented here:

PEEVISH → PRANK → POUT → *PISS*

This can, and too often does, result in Paddling:

PEEVISH → PRANK → POUT → PISS → *PADDLE*

It may appear that by such Paddling the owner has Prevailed. Wrong. The cat has yet another move. Of its bowels. In the pot with the houseplant, or some place that's not appropriate. As in:

PEEVISH → PRANK → POUT → PISS → PADDLE → *POOP*

Here we see that the cat wins—or *would* win if we resorted to Paddling. Remember our admonition to *DO NO HARM*, because we would then experience *OWNER GUILT*, which the goddam cat will add to its arsenal of grievances for future use against the owner who otherwise takes good care of it.

Consult this chart any time you want to play *Kick the Cat*.

THE CAT-BATH

Among the many things cats don't like is water, except maybe to drink. What they *really* don't like is

getting a bath. This spares the cat's owner the hassles that go with dogs, who like water and bathing because they can shake themselves off, and you can't. Still, to heed a cat's anti-water attitude is to deny its owner the hilarity of seeing a cat that's *soaking wet*.

As funny as cats look when wet (especially long-haired cats that overthink their visuals), hosing one down purely for amusement is not the mark of a kindly cat owner. Nor should a cat owner infest his cat with fleas just to give it a flea bath. But a soaked-and-soaped cat is definitely called for in the September/October 1990 issue of *In Health* magazine, which carries an article about cats who cause allergic reactions. The article says that people with cat allergies are reacting to a protein called *Fel d-1*, which is excreted by the cat equivalent of sweat-glands onto the cat equivalent of dandruff.

This may not be applicable in the case of married cat owners whose spouses don't sneeze a lot, but the unmarried cat owner may see cat-bathing as a form of preventative

> **Furry jury turns up noses at certain Soviet sausage**
>
> ASSOCIATED PRESS
>
> MOSCOW — Angry meatpackers are suing a newspaper for an article that said their sausage was so bad that even cats can't stomach it; but

medicine—one that results in a *non-allergenic* cat that can't be used as your first date's cheap excuse for refusing to spend the night.

THE CAT AND THE BALLOON

First you get a balloon. Not the heavy-duty kiddie-type balloon like you buy in a toy store, but a drugstore condom made from very thin latex. Find a cute girl employee, wink lasciviously, then in a loud whisper say, *Got any rubbers?*

Just kidding.

With drugstore condoms, you don't want a Trojan with its fancy ribs and colors and its no-knock-'em-up quality control. You want one of the twenty-five-cent kind, like you pull off a shelf-display.[23] Then you

---

23. If you're a boy, ignore that look of disapproval you get from the pharmacist. If you're a girl, claim you teach sex education and need one for a cucumber.

take said rubber, blow it up to the max, and place it somewhere in kitty range. Presuming your cat has passed the attention-getting test, it will think, *"What the hell is that? I think I'll take a look."*

Once Mr. Cat looks and decides to paw, Mr. Balloon will go Pop! Then Mr. Cat will loft in the air, eyes wide and hair a-bristle.

This works only once. As they say, a cat bitten by a snake won't go near a rope.[24]

WATER PISTOL ETIQUETTE

Considering the antipathy cats have for water, only a sadist would squirt his cat with a water pistol. That is to say, only a sadist would *enjoy* squirting his cat with a water pistol.

However, the enlightened cat owner, who would never consider paddling his cat, but who understands the need for lesser forms of discipline, may find the water-pistol an alternative to corporal punishment.

Spare the rod[25] and spoil the cat, in other words.

The cat owner who goes out and buys a quart-capacity, battery-operated, fully-automatic water-gun styled like an M-16, or who would cut loose on his cat with a garden hose, should not be encouraged. In fact, he should not be encouraged to even have a cat.

So for cat-wetting purposes a modest little 39-cent water pistol will do nicely. We are not in some Commie

---

24. I think I already said that.
25. Unless the rod is a handgun.

police state, after all, where even non-violent protests and requests for human rights are met with barbarous repression, like at Tienanmen Square. Hell no. The only purpose of our water-pistol therapy is to alert our cat to one penalty for misbehavior.

Because that's hard to explain to a cat you should *sneak* the water-pistol into play and squirt it at the whining, nagging, demanding cat only when its back is turned. This way the cat is not sure where the squirt of water came from and will think *God did it.*[26]

THE VACUUM CLEANER

The Good Lord was not thinking of cats when He gave us the vacuum cleaner.[27] That, or He, too, has a sense of humor. For the vacuum cleaner is the creature's natural enemy. It is the one best thing that gives cat owners power over the feline kingdom. It alone penetrates the cat's facade of boredom by creating a conflict between its logical brain, which tells it to *be cool,* and its nervous system, which tells it *Chainsaw Killer, Coming After Me!*

To ram a howling Hoover at a cornered cat would amuse only a sadist and must never enter the reader's mind.[28] Instead, we should start our machine in another room and introduce it to our cat slowly, in a nonthreatening manner; we want this to

Mike Royko

Appetite for cats is purely cultural

In a society as ethnically and racially diverse as ours, there are bound to be occasional cultural misunderstandings.

As an example, consider the recent case of the man, the cat and the cop in Tulsa.

An off-duty policeman was sitting home one day when he got a phone call from a neighbor.

The neighbor said that she saw something strange—a man walking down the street carrying a cat by its neck. The cat appeared to be unhappy.

The cop hopped in his car and drove a couple of blocks. Sure enough, there was a man—later identified as one Huy Van Nguyen—with a plump cat. But now he was carrying the cat by its hind legs.

Since this isn't the way cats are usually handled, the policeman became suspicious. So he

---

26. God, however, should not overdue it.

27. You don't have a vacuum cleaner? Borrow one, or run back and forth with a stick, humming mournfully.

28. "The Devil made me do it!" is not an acceptable excuse.

be a growth experience.[29]

Figure that an otherwise well-adjusted cat won't panic at the sound of a vacuum. It will merely open an eyelid one or two millimeters, bump its Alert status up to Yellow, and await further developments. The gradual approach of the machine may flip the nerve switch from fright to flight, but a particularly stubborn cat may resist movement as long as the vacuum isn't visible. And here is where the fun (let's call it training) comes in.

Enter the room slowly with the usual push-and-pull, inching the machine closer and closer to our pretending-to-sleep cat. When its courage curve intersects with its anxiety curve, its indecision will turn into consternation and pussy will surrender to cowardice. When that happens, our pet will vanish in a slinking trot, exhibiting none of the grace or guts that might have saved kitty-cat from looking like a whipped pup.

BACKING YOUR CAT

Teaching your cat to walk backwards may not be much of a trick, except to the cat, but it's no trick at all. Just find a paper sack that will fit over pussy's head, and so long as it resists a shake-off, your cat will walk backwards.

This may be your lowest bid yet for immortality, but if you never amount to anything, it will be everything, and everybody should do something they'll be remembered by.

---

29. The noise of a vacuum cleaner travels for miles and the sound of one will fill our cat with the anxiety known to a soldier, hunkered down in a foxhole, whose ears pick up the clanking and skreaking of an approaching enemy tank.

CATCRAFT

Most of us rather like our cats to have a streak of wickedness. I should not feel quite easy in the company of any cat that walked about the house with a saintly expression.

— Beverly Nichols

PETS FOR YOUR PET

Squeamish folks who are fastidious housekeepers are denying their cats the mental stimulation of pursuing mice and high-velocity insects. They are also likely to deprive their pets of the white mice they can buy at any pet store, or the goldfish that will invite their kitty to wet its paw, or the canary-bird it can terrorize until the feathers fall off.

The result can be a cat whose predatory instincts and hunting skills grow rusty from disuse, especially if it's an Apartment Cat. To compensate for the lack of excitement the loving owner should consider purchasing an ant farm.

ANT FARM

For a cat with no back yard in which to hunt, no kitchen that attracts roaches, no pet bird to drool at hungrily, no bowl of goldfish in which to troll, can still derive hours of entertainment from an ant farm, as should be apparent to anyone who has watched pussy obsess over insects it cannot catch. Indeed, the average Apartment Cat will spend hours gazing in crossed-eyed bliss at any tiny creature that may be trapped by circumstance but stays in play.

Having its own ant farm, brimful of crawling, wiggling, energetic morsels sandwiched behind clear

plastic is the cat's equivalent of television—television that you yourself might find boring, unless you are into ants.

CATS AS ANTIDEPRESSANTS

Neurologists have discovered that owning a pet helps many people deal with their emotional disorders. The Three Dog Night, which kept our pioneers warm in bed, can be prescribed as tranquilizers, and the Three Cat Night as No Doze. More recently dogs have been prescribed for PTSD and cats as antidepressants.

Especially for men who are heartbroken over the loss of a girlfriend.[30] Women, being *ipso facto* more emotionally involved, if they lose a boyfriend, who isn't,

---

30. At least until the girlfriend takes up with another man—another man who purports to be thoughtful, considerate, and committed to the relationship, when you know it's only his strategy for getting laid!

can take the matter up with her girlfriends, which a boy can't. I'm not sure where I was going with this.

Anyway, the therapeutic value of cats in the treatment of depression varies with the number of cats and the severity of the depression. Their effectiveness probably depends on how nuts one is about cats.

How safe is the use of cats for affective mood disorders? Only one adverse side effect has been recorded.

Adverse Event or Condition	Percentage Reporting	
	Prozac	Cat
Headache	20.3	0
Nervousness	14.9	0
Insomnia	13.8	0
Drowsiness	11.6	0
Anxiety	9.4	0
Tremor	7.9	0
Dizziness	5.7	0
Fatigue	4.0	0
Mouth dryness	9.5	0
Libido decreased	3.1	0
Sexual dysfunction	9.1	0
Hot flashes	1.8	N/A
Palpitations	1.3	0
Menstrual Complaint	1.9	N/A
Asthenia	4.4	0
Constipation	4.5	0
Vomiting	2.4	0
Hairballs	0	98.7

This chart is by Bubba Bohunk who thinks doctors still prescribe Prozac.

DID OUR BOOT CAMP DO ITS JOB?

If, after these exercises, your cat still refuses to romp and frolic, if it only slumbers and licks itself, if it doesn't respond to simple requests, if it looks at you with boredom and annoyance, it is either shirking its duties or faking it, in which case:

- Smile real big, drag out the cat carrier, and say something like, *How would kitty like to go for a little ride?* If the cat bounds off and goes into hiding, we have a cat that is shamming.

- If the vet threat doesn't work, multiply the cat's age by seven... Wait. That's dog years. Go find a cat book (all mine are in boxes).

THE
MAXIM SILENCER

Splendid for Noisy Cats

"I want to tell you how your Silencer helps us keep house. We live in a big apartment house and there are neighboring back yards which are regular battle fields for cats. These half wild creatures nightly get into political arguments which disturb us so much we lose sleep.

My wife, who is a nervous invalid, but nevertheless gifted with a fine working imagination, suggested to me that I buy a Maxim Silencer and shoot the troublesome animals. Being something of an outdoor man and fond of hunting, the idea struck me as pretty good. I bought a Silencer for my little Remington, and put it on easily—thanks to the little coupling which came with it.

The first night after getting the thing fixed up I had a good chance to use it. We had retired and were just getting to sleep when a couple of cats started up. I immediately got up, and finally located them right down on the grass of a yard. Knowing the little .22 short cartridge would be perfectly safe fired into the grass and earth from above, I got out the little rifle and with considerable excitement got a bead on the biggest one of the cats. I pulled the trigger, there was a little click and the old cat went end over end a couple of times and then lay still. The other cat paused a moment and then withdrew in haste, and we were left in quiet.

I suppose the people who found the dead cat put it in the ash barrel for me. It is great having your game retrieved this way. Since then I have done away with just ten cats who have disturbed our sleep at night. Instead of being in trouble all the time over the noise, we now have quiet nights or the means to make them quiet if they get noisy.

Anyone understanding how to shoot safely, and living in a neighborhood where cats are troublesome, ought to get a little .22 cal. rifle and a Maxim Silencer without delay."

A. L. M.

Rifle   Coupling   Silencer

READING ASSIGNMENTS

*Consciousness-raising material
on collateral issues*

THE INTELLIGENCE OF CATS
By Michael Joseph

The cat is a peculiarly sensitive and, if you like, temperamental animal. You can learn nothing about him unless you first establish friendly relations, and that takes time, sympathy, and patience. He is easily frightened [but] cannot be intimidated. Everyone who has made a close study of cats knows how a cat will isolate himself if there is any attempt at arbitrary procedure. For this reason it is rarely possible to teach a cat even the elemental repetitive tricks which monkeys, dogs, and some other animals learn with ease and sometimes with relish. To my mind, this merely proves that the cat is unwilling to obey. The assumption that he does not *understand* what is required of him seems to me quite untenable.

What would constitute a fair test of the cat's intelligence? Before attempting to answer the question let me first offer some general observations. It is impossible to understand cats on the strength of superficial acquaintance. They are shy, unobtrusive creatures who prefer solitude to uncongenial company. Unlike dogs, they are not anxious to make a good impression. In the cat's personality there is aloofness, pride, and a profound dignity. Even the most ordinary cat has a touch of the aristocrat.

The cat does not wish to be understood. The

How to Outsmart Your Cat

blandishments of other and more sociable animals are not in his line. If human beings are so foolish as to regard him as the social inferior of the dog, a convenient mouse-trap and nothing else, the cat's philosophy is proof against such injustice. He goes his own way, blandly indifferent to human folly. It is not his business to correct it.

Above all, the cat is independent. If he choose he will follow you around, play with you, demonstrate his affection; but try to exact obedience from a cat and you will immediately find it is not forthcoming. Even Siamese cats, which are more responsive than other breeds, will refuse to do what they are told. If I say to my dog, "Come here" he comes. I have not the slightest doubt that my cat understands me but, unless he feels like it, I can summon him in vain.

This reluctance to obey—call it perversity if you will—is responsible for the common lack of appreciation of the cat. His disregard of us and our wishes is disagreeably unflattering. The trouble is that we human beings are so vain that we look upon the habits of any domestic animal (of course the cat is not truly domesticated) as being specially developed for our benefit. The dog or monkey that will learn mechanical tricks for the reward of a pat on the head or a piece of sugar is acclaimed for his skill. And this ability to understand *and obey* is applauded as a sign of intelligence.

The cat, on the other hand, applies his skill and intelligence to his own purposes. There is truth in Bernard Shaw's remark that footballers' brains are in their feet. The cat reveals its braininess by incredibly skillful feats of jumping and balancing, but it is useless commanding him to perform. The rarity of performing cats is significant.

Anyone who has much experience with cats will agree that it is temperamentally incapable of obedience....

To be logical, it is not truly intelligent of the horse to carry loads or to pull a heavy cart; nor is it intelligent of the monkey to ape human mannerisms; or of the dog to fetch and carry or perform clownish antics for his owner's satisfaction. It may be very amusing but it is typical of human vanity that we should so often hail as intelligence what is merely gratifying— and unreasoning—obedience to our whims.

Here is the definition I offer of animal intelligence: an animal's ability to reason and act for itself, in any situation which may arise in its experience, without human interference.

Judged by this standard, the cat, as I hope to satisfy the reader, passes with distinction. If there is one opportunist in the animal world, it is our friend the cat. He is independent, resourceful, even cunning. He lives on its wits.

Cats are often, with justification, I admit, accused of selfishness—a trait which frequently reveals intelligence. The choicest morsels of food, the cosiest place by the fireside, liberty to come and go when he likes— all these are signs of intelligent appreciation at least.

It is obvious that the cat lover may overestimate his favorite's intelligence. Parents are notoriously proud, gardeners may boast of their blooms, anglers exaggerate their captures; and the animal lover is apt in his enthusiasm to endow his pet with qualities it does not really possess. It is dangerously easy to endow an intelligent-looking animal with human motives and reasoning powers. Cat lovers are fallible. Like the rest.

Yet I maintain that it is possible to distinguish the cat's intelligence by careful observation.

My tortoiseshell tabby, Minna Minna Mowbray, was playing one day with her kittens by the door off a balcony which overlooked my garden. I noticed she was dragging along a piece of meat, brought from the kitchen downstairs. She was quite obviously using it

How to Outsmart Your Cat

as a plaything and, as it was covered with hairs from the carpet, I took it from her without thinking, opened the door leading onto the balcony, and threw it out into the garden below. I saw—but Minna did not—that it landed in a clump of bushes. She looked up at me reproachfully, then without hesitation ran downstairs. In a few seconds she was out in the garden, hunting for the meat. Now to get into the garden she had to go down two flights of stairs, through a basement and scullery and out of the door at the back of the house.

What would a less intelligent animal have done? A dog, I suspect, would have barked protestingly and jumped up to look over the balcony railing but I doubt if it would have immediately occurred to him that there was only one way to recover his property and that was to go down to the garden and search for it. It took my cat only a few minutes to find the meat and bring it upstairs again.

—*Harpers, May, 1935*

ROLFING YOUR CAT
By Michael Stanborough
Certified Rolfer, Austin, Texas

Students of the healing arts are generally aware that modern medicine, as practiced by physicians and veterinarians, draws heavily upon discoveries in biological chemistry over the past 125 or so years. Such medicine is called "allopathic," treating as it does the symptoms of disease by means of drugs that discomfort cats at least as much as humans, who also don't like having needles stuck in them.

The alternative to terrifying veterinarian visits is mechanical or manipulative medicine, which requires no special equipment and can be performed in the home.

A brief examination of the various treatments that are more or less holistic—including the chiropractic, homeopathic, naturopathic and yoga — suggests that the one from which your pet is most likely to benefit from is the creative variation on massage and manipulation therapy known as Rolfing, which tones body and mind simultaneously.

Named for Dr. Ida Rolf who popularized the treatment at the Eselen Institute in California in the 1970s, Rolfing involves both manipulation and exercise aimed at integrating and aligning the body's infrastructure, as it were. The myofascial or connective tissue system at the joints makes the cat's internal structure a very resilient, plastic, elastic medium that can be changed by *adding energy through physical pressure*. The resulting change in structure produces a change in function, according to a principle tenent of Rolfing.

Thus, when the myofascial tissue at boney interfaces is pulled, pushed, twisted, turned, jerked, stretched, gouged, yanked, thumped, and otherwise repositioned, the bones themselves spontaneously reorient and the organism becomes "balanced." This produces a feeling of warmth and expansion and well-being—probably like hitting one's head with a hammer because it feels so good when you stop.

A properly Rolfed cat will come out of the experience a completely integrated cat, virtually a new cat with a new attitude, boundless energy and all-around kittenish behavior, especially when it hears you say the word "Rolf!"

DOES YOUR CAT CAUSE BRAIN DAMAGE?

By Tamara Shaffer

Plus an interview with movie critic Thisbe

Do cats cause brain damage?

The possibility that cat owners suffer brain damage from cats has not been fully explored by a scientific community that, unfortunately, more often causes brain damage *to* cats. The fact that some cat owners seem not to behave rationally is insufficient to establish cause and effect, for no comparison studies have been made of the same cat owners with the cat factored out.

However, there is anecdotal evidence that cats, if they do not cause brain damage, cause some owners to exhibit what could be mistaken for it.

For instance, one Chicago cat owner watches movies partly from the perspective of her cat Thisbe and then puts herself in Thisbe's place to write a review of the movie for the cat community.

She is not crazy. She does this simply as a means of exercising an active imagination and creative impulses that are not part of her job description and, if too long pent up, would probably get her into trouble of one sort or another. Thus, we have here an interesting case where the very existence of the cat helps its owner maintain at least a tentative grip on her sanity in the face of reality.

Whether her cat knows it or not.

The fact that Thisbe never gets to see the movies it reviews (unless they come to television) is immaterial. For Ms. L.J., movie-reviewing is an art in itself and an end in itself, and insofar as she has no newspaper or magazine column or TV program through which to reach the general movie-going public, L. J. and her cat Thisbe have had a convenient closed-circuit system by which they could privately amuse one another without humiliation or embarrassment.

Until now.

The following review of *Fatal Attraction* has been supplied by Lorel Janizewski on the condition that she remain anonymous.

AT THE MEOWVIES
By Thisbe

Fatal Attraction is a major hit with humans despite the notable absence of any cat. Consequently, its appeal is limited. There is a typically obedient, playful dog and an inconsequential rabbit who dies sans funeral, so it is difficult to understand what the film is trying to say. At one level it is an advertisement for fidelity, using scare tactics. The Man (Michael Douglas) is away from his family one night—*one night*—and BOOM he is having an affair with Another Woman (Glenn Close). His dog joins the illicit duo in playful activity the next day and doesn't even mess in the house to show his disapproval.

The Woman turns out to be a crazy, lonely person, possibly for want of a cat. She makes the man's life a living hell, wreaking havoc on all members of his family, including the rabbit.

Typical of films addressed to humans, the moral tactics are questionable. When a cat does something "wrong" but "natural," like messing on the floor or shredding the sofa, it must answer to its partner (i.e., "owner"). An accommodation must be reached. This may be in the form of more freedom for the cat to roam outside in return for laying off the sofa and not messing on the floor. Giving Douglas more freedom to roam might have satisfied his half of the equation, but the negative impact such mating has on his partner, when he is caught—*and he is caught only because the "other woman" is mentally unbalanced!*—results in his punishment for the wrong reasons. In a sense, Douglas roamed and, in doing so, *also* messed on the floor, which clouds the moral issues involved.

But the movie isn't about morality. It's about water. Lots of water, boiling and dripping and drowning. On that level, it is a horror movie, and I give it only one star.

TOILET CLEANING INSTRUCTIONS
From Jerry Chastain

1. Put both lids of the toilet up and add 1/8 cup of pet shampoo to the water in the bowl.
2. Pick up the cat, soothe him, and carry him to the bathroom.
3. In one smooth movement, put the cat in the toilet and close both lids. You may need to stand on the lid.
4. The cat will self-agitate and make ample suds. Never mind the noises that come from the toilet; the cat is actually enjoying this.
5. Flush the toilet three or four times. This provides a "power-wash" and rinse.
6. Have someone open the front door of your home. Be sure that there are no people between the bathroom and the front door.

7. Stand behind the toilet as far as you can and quickly lift both lids.
8. The cat will rocket out of the toilet, streak out of the bathroom, and lick himself till he's dry.
9. Both the commode and the cat will be sparkling clean.

———————

NOTE: The following list was evidently the work of some feline pedagogue instructing younger cats on the Do's and Don'ts of cathood. And one one his pupils, being an adolescent, ignored his admonition about confidentiality and left it beside its pallet.

HOUSE RULES

DOORS: Do not allow closed doors in any room. To get door opened, stand on hind legs and hammer with forepaws. Once door is opened, it is not necessary to use it. After you have ordered an outside door opened, stand halfway in and out and think about several things. This is particularly important during cold weather, rain, snow, or mosquito season. Swinging doors are to be avoided at all costs.

BATHROOMS: Always accompany guests to the bathroom. It is not necessary to do anything—just sit and stare.

HAMPERING: If one of your humans is engaged in some activity and the other is idle, stay with the busy one. This is called helping, otherwise known as hampering. Following are the rules for hampering:

a) It is beneath the Dignity of a cat

How to Outsmart Your Cat

to beg food as lower forms of life (such as dogs) will, but several techniques exist for ensuring that the humans don't forget you exist. These include, but are not limited to: jumping onto the lap and purring loudly; lying down in the doorway between the dining room and the kitchen; the Direct Stare; and twining around people's legs as they sit and eat while meowing plaintively.

b) When a human is holding the newspaper in front of him/her, be sure to jump on the back of the paper. They also love to jump.

c) When supervising cooking, sit just behind the left heel of the cook. You cannot be seen and thereby stand a better chance of being stepped on and then picked up and comforted.

d) For book readers, get in close under the chin, between eyes and book, unless you can lie across the book itself.

e) For knitting projects or paperwork, lie on the work in the most appropriate manner so as to obscure as much of the work or at least the most important part. Pretend to doze, but every so often reach out and slap the pencil or knitting needles. The worker may try to distract you; ignore it. Remember, the aim is to hamper work. Embroidery and needlepoint projects make great hammocks in spite of what the humans may tell you.

f) For people paying bills (monthly activity) or working on income taxes or Christmas cards (annual activities), keep in mind the aim—to hamper! First, sit on the paper being worked on. When dislodged, watch sadly from the side of the table. When activity proceeds, roll around on the papers, scattering them to the best of your ability. After being removed for the second time, push pens, pencils, and erasers off the table, one at a time.

WALKING: As often as possible, dart quickly and as close as possible in front of the human, especially: on stairs, when they have something in their arms, in the dark, and when they first get up in the morning. This will help their coordination skills.

PLAY: This is an important part of your life. Get enough sleep in the daytime so you are ready for your nocturnal games. Below are listed several favorite cat games that you can play. It is important though to maintain one's Dignity at all times. If you should have an accident during play, such as falling off a chair, immediately wash a part of your body as if to say I MEANT to do that! It fools those humans every time.

KING OF THE HILL: This game must be played with at least one other cat. The more, the merrier! One or both of the sleeping humans is Hill 303 which must be defended at all costs from the other cat(s). Anything goes. This game allows for the development of unusual tactics as one must take the unstable playing theater into account.

WARNING: Playing either of these games to excess will result in expulsion from the bed and possibly from the bedroom. Should the humans grow restless, immediately begin purring and cuddle up to them. This should buy you some time until they fall asleep again. If one happens to be on a human when this occurs, this cat wins the round of King of the Hill.

TOYS: Any small item is a potential toy. If a human tries to confiscate it, this means that it is a Good Toy. Run with it under the bed. Look suitably outraged when the human grabs you and takes it away. Always watch where it is put so you can steal it later.

SLEEPING: It is usually not difficult to find a comfortable place to curl up. Any place a human likes to sit is good, especially if it contrasts with your fur color. If it's in a sunbeam or near a heating duct or radiator, so much the better. Of course, good places also exist outdoors, but have the disadvantages of being seasonal and dependent on weather conditions.

SCRATCHING POSTS: Humans are very protective of what they think is their property and will object strongly if they catch you sharpening your claws on it. Doing it when they aren't around won't help, as they are very observant. Sharpening your claws on a human is not advisable.

HUMANS: Humans have three functions: to feed us, to play with and give attention to us, and to empty the litter-box. It is important to maintain one's Dignity when around humans so that they will not forget who is the master.

———————

THE CAT AND THE LAW
By Harry Hibschman

"For a dog to chase, frighten, annoy, and worry a cat," said the highest court of the State of Connecticut in 1901, "is to do the cat a mischief."

Speaking with equal wisdom and assurance, Judge Higgins of Tennessee said in 1914: "There is a natural. antipathy between the cat and the dog. The very presence of a cat in the wake of a dog is a challenge, an insult, a bait, and an enticement. Fido will run after Thomas."

Such being the facts of natural science as judicially determined, and neighbors being still weak of spirit, prone to anger and to take up arms for the vindication of the rights of their pets, the question naturally arises, What are the rights and liabilities of Thomas?

The legal status of the cat has had a varied history. We find that there was a time under the common law when to steal a cat was not larceny for the reason that a cat was not considered to have any intrinsic value. This was true also of the dog and resulted in an anomalous situation: a man might be prosecuted for stealing the skin of a dead cat or dog though he would go scot free if he stole the live animal. Blackstone, that patron saint of the law, laid down the rule that animals not fit for food, or base, or kept only for pleasure, curiosity, or whim, could not be the subject of larceny.

That, however, was not the law among the ancient Britons. They specifically regarded certain cats as the "guardians of the King's granary" and provided that any person who killed one of them should be punished by having to deliver to the King an amount of wheat measured by the size of the cat, or at least by

How to Outsmart Your Cat

its length. To determine this amount the law provided, "Let the cat be hung up by the tip of its tail with its head touching the floor, and let grains of wheat be poured upon it until the extremity of its tail be covered with the wheat." The amount of wheat required to do that was the amount that the offender had to deliver as a penalty.

The law came to be changed by the courts, so the authorities say, when larceny was made punishable with death and the judges tried to mitigate the severities of the law. In later years it was changed, again, both in England and in most of the States of this country, either by statute or by judicial decision, so that now cats are looked upon, as the Supreme Judicial Court of Maine said some years ago, as "things of value" and the subject of larceny. Or as the Supreme Court of Georgia expressed it a number of years ago: "The ancient idea that 'animals which do not serve for food, and which therefore the law holds to have no intrinsic value' were not subject to larceny, has passed away. Now the stomach is not the only criterion of value."

Cats are classified technically as animals *mansuetae naturae* as opposed to animals *ferae naturae,* that is to say, as animals tame by nature or animals that "come to the hand," as distinguished from animals wild by nature. That the cat—speaking of course of the household cat and not of cats like the lion and the tiger—is properly placed in the first of these two classes is evident from its long and respectable history as well as from common experience. As the Supreme Judicial Court of Maine expressed it: "The time of its domestication is lost in the mists of time, but it is apparent that the cat was a domestic animal among the early Egyptians, by whom it came to be regarded as sacred, as evidenced by the device of Cambyses during his invasion of Egypt, B.C. 525 or 527, which could scarcely have been feasible if the animal had been wild. From that day to this it has been a dweller in the houses of men. In no other animal has affection for home been more strongly developed, and in none, when absent from home, can the *animus revertendi* be more surely assumed to exist."

Turning to some typical cases involving cats before the law, we may as well begin with the traditional one of the cat and the canary, for, believe it or not, such a case was actually brought before a Pennsylvania court for decision more than fifty years ago and seems to be the earliest cat case reported in our American books of the law.

The plaintiff in that case alleged and undertook to prove that the defendant was the owner of a cat which on a certain day wandered off the home grounds in search of adventure, invaded the premises of the plaintiff, and then and there pounced upon, caught, killed, and carried away one canary of great value belonging to the plaintiff, to his damage in a sum not mentioned in the report of the case. The basis of the court's decision and the court's conclusion are shown in the following quotation, which, it will be noted, reveals a considerable amount of judicial knowledge of cats: "Cats attach themselves to places rather than persons and are rather harbored than owned. They are not subject to direction like dogs, nor can they be put under the same restraint as other domestic animals. To some extent they may be regarded as still undomesticated, and their predatory habits as but a remnant of their wild nature. The depredations which they commit in their wanderings are to be ascribed to this and may be compared to the damages done by other animals of a partially wild nature... The record shows no cause of action against the defendant."

An English court reached precisely the same conclusion a few years ago in a case involving numerous feline raids on a pigeon roost, holding that the owner of the 'cat found guilty of committing the

How to Outsmart Your Cat

dastardly acts was not liable under the law for the value of the pigeons taken unless he had notice of what was going on. It was not negligence, the court held, to permit a cat to follow its natural bent to prowl, nor was the owner liable as a matter of course simply because the cat was a trespasser upon the close or property of another.

This question of the cat as a trespasser was presented in this country in another case decided some twenty years ago. The cat in that case had bitten the plaintiff while away from its home premises, and it was earnestly argued that that fact alone was sufficient to establish the liability of the owner. But the highest court of Connecticut, before whom this case eventually came, said of that contention, "No negligence can be attributed to the mere trespass of a cat which has neither mischievous nor vicious propensities."

The court in that case also wrote a fine testimonial for the cat, saying: "The cat is not of a species of animals naturally inclined to mischief, such as, for example, cattle, whose instinct is to rove and whose practice is to eat and trample down growing crops. The cat's disposition is kindly and docile, and by nature it is one of the most tame and harmless of all domestic animals."

Nor does the fact that a cat's disposition is not quite so angelic when it has kittens make its owner liable for damages to a person bitten by the cat. That at least was the ruling of an English court about twenty-five years ago in a case in which a woman had brought suit against the owner of a cat for damages inflicted by the animal. The facts in the case as brought out at the trial were substantially these: The woman, accompanied by a small dog, entered a little shop kept by the owner of the cat, the latter with her kittens being at the time in a closet or alcove opening off the shop. While the woman looked at some of the objects displayed for sale and talked to the proprietor, she permitted the dog to follow its own canine inclinations, and they led him promptly toward the spot occupied by the mother cat and her kittens. The cat, taking due notice of the approach of one of her natural and hereditary enemies and believing no doubt, and justly, that he came with evil intent, launched a sudden attack, without a previous declaration of war, and promptly fell upon the dog with such fury that it howled with terror and sought refuge in the arms of its mistress. Infuriated and nothing daunted, the cat followed and tried to reach its foe even there. The result was that while the dog tried to protect itself and the woman tried to protect her pet, the cat failed to discriminate between dog and mistress and scratched and bit the latter on both arms and in several other places not specifically described in the reports of the case.

It was for the injuries thus inflicted by the cat that the owner of the dog brought suit against the owner of the cat. The court, however, found itself unable to grant her any relief, holding that, even though the cat, ordinarily kind and gentle, was inclined to be savage, particularly toward dogs, while moved by the maternal spirit, that fact did not remove it from the class of animals recognized as *mansuetae naturae*. Its owner was, therefore, held not liable to the owner of the dog.

In this case of course the dog entered into the picture, and both he and his mistress were the losers. But it may be different where the dog comes out the victor. In the Tennessee case already mentioned, for instance, Judge Higgins seemed to think that there was a doctrine of self-defense as applicable in the case of a dog as in the case of a man. At any rate this is what he said: "The court is satisfied that on the particular night in question, when Thomas Cat approached the path down which Speed (the villain dog) was traveling, he bowed his back and growled and spit in the dog's face. This was necessarily a felonious and a 'felineous' assault on the part of the cat, and the dog had the right, undoubtedly, to make such return as was necessary to protect himself from serious bodily harm at the hands of his long-clawed antagonist."

That this doctrine of self-defense prevails also in favor of the cat, at least by proxy, is the manifest result of the ruling in the Maine case already referred to. For the question involved there was whether the owner of a cat had the right to kill a foxhound that had chased the cat back home and followed it onto the home premises with evident intent to do the cat serious bodily harm; and it was held that the summary execution of the dog was justified under a statute which read: "Any person may lawfully kill a dog which is found worrying, wounding, or killing any domestic animal, when said dog is outside of the enclosure or immediate care of its owner or keeper."

The earlier Connecticut case previously referred to involved similar facts, but the conclusion of the court was different. The dog in that case had also chased the cat back home, but the cat had reached a place of safety in a tree before its owner had appeared on the scene and shot the dog to death. The Connecticut law applicable to the case permitted the killing of a dog for the protection of life or property; but the court held that the owner of the cat was liable for the value of the dog because it had not really been necessary for him to kill the dog in order to protect the cat, since the cat had already found a safe retreat in the tree when the dog was killed.

The sum and substance of it all is, then, that the cat is in perfectly good standing under the law in our day as a domestic animal, an animal *mansuetae naturae,* a thing of value, and the subject of larceny; that, unless there is evidence of the known vicious disposition of a particular cat, its owner is not liable for its trespass upon the premises of another nor for injuries inflicted by it, either upon feathered victims or persons; and that, while the law recognizes a dog's right of self-defense, ordinarily the owner of a cat has a legal right to protect his cat against a dog, at least against a trespassing dog, with such force as may be adequate to the circumstances, even to the extent of taking the dog's life.

If any cat owner objects that I have not answered all the pertinent questions that occur to him in connection with my immediate subject, I can only plead that I have covered all those passed upon by the courts, to the best of my knowledge. And, if it later develops that I was wrong in any of my conclusions, I now enter my excuse in advance in the words of an English judge, namely and to wit: "God forbid that it should be imagined that an attorney, or a counsel, or even a judge, is bound to know all the law."

—Harper's, September, 1936.

LAW & ORDER

I cannot agree that it should be the declared policy of Illinois that a cat visiting a neighbor's yard or crossing the highway is a public nuisance. It is the nature of cats to do a certain amount of unescorted roaming. Many live with their owners in apartments or other restricted premises, and I doubt if we want to make their every brief foray an opportunity for a small game hunt by zealous citizens — with traps or otherwise.

I am afraid this bill could only create discord, recrimination, and enmity.

Also consider the owner's dilemma: To escort a cat abroad on a leash is against the nature of a cat, and to permit it to venture forth for exercise unattended

How to Outsmart Your Cat

into a night of new dangers is against the nature of the owner.

Moreover, cats perform useful service, particularly in rural areas, in combatting rodents—work they necessarily perform alone and without regard for property lines.

We are all interested in protecting certain varieties of bird. That cats destroy some birds, I well know, but I believe this legislation would further but little the worthy cause to which its proponents give such unselfish effort. The problem of cat versus bird is as old as time. If we attempt to resolve it by legislation, who knows but what we may be called upon to take sides as well in the age-old problems of dog versus cat, bird versus bird, or even bird versus worm.

In my opinion, the State of Illinois and its local governing bodies already have enough to do without trying to control feline delinquency.

> — *Illinois Gov. Adlai Stevenson,*
> *vetoing cat-control legislation*

Any person over the age of twenty-one years possessing a hunting license may, and game protectors and other peace officers shall, humanely destroy cats at large found hunting or killing any bird protected by law, or with a dead bird of any species protected by law in its possession, and no action for damages shall lie for such killing.

> — *New York State Conservation Law*

CATQUOTES

Compared to dogs, whose owners describe them in terms rhapsodic, cats get a bum rap. They are usually depicted as contrary, conniving, smarter, often evil. I do not subscribe to those sentiments nor do I bear cats any ill will, to speak of.

—Anonymous

Cats are smarter than dogs. You can't get eight cats to pull a sled through the snow.

—Jeff Valdez

Cats are poetry in motion. Dogs are gibberish in neutral.

—Anonymous

Thousands of years ago, cats were worshiped as gods. Cats have never forgotten this.

—Anonymous

Cats are rather delicate creatures and they are subject to a good many ailments, but I never heard of one who suffered from insomnia.

—Joseph Wood Krutch

People who hate cats will come back as mice in their next life.

—Faith Resnick

The cat, having sat upon a hot stove lid, will not sit upon a hot stove lid again. Nor upon a cold stove lid.

—Mark Twain

The man who carries a cat by the tail learns something that can be learned in no other way.

—*Mark Twain*

Cats have nine lives. Which makes them ideal for experimentation.

—*Anonymous*

Dogs come when they're called; cats take a message and get back to you later.

—*Mary Bly*

My husband said it was either him or the cat. I miss him sometimes.

—*Anonymous*

The mice that find themselves between the cats' teeth acquire no merit from their sacrifices.

—*Mahatma Gandhi*

I gave my cat a bath the other day. They love it. He just sat there and enjoyed it. It was fun for me. The fur would stick to my tongue, but other than that....

—*Steve Martin*

Cats are intended to teach us that not everything in nature has a purpose.

—*Garrison Keillor*

Some people say that cats are sneaky, evil, and cruel. True, and they have many other fine qualities as well.

—*Missy Dizick*

Women and cats will do as they please. Men and dogs should relax and get used to this.

—*Anonymous*

How to Outsmart Your Cat

Cats are notoriously sore losers. Coming in second best, especially to someone as poorly coordinated as a human being, grates their sensibility.

—*Stephen Baker*

The fog comes on little cat feet. It sits looking over harbor and city on silent haunches and then, moves on.

—*Carl Sandburg*

A cat, I am sure, could walk on a cloud without coming through.

—*Jules Verne*

A kitten is a rosebud in the garden of the animal kingdom.

—*Robert Southey*

The clever cat eats cheese and breathes down rat holes with baited breath.

—*W. C. Fields*

Cat: A pygmy lion who loves mice, hates dogs and patronizes human beings.

—*Oliver Herford*

There is no snooze button on a cat who wants breakfast.

—*Anonymous*

Managing senior programmers is like herding cats.

—*Dave Platt*

Kitten: A small homicidal muffin on legs; affects human sensibilities to the point of endowing the most wanton and ruthless acts of destruction with near-mythical overtones of cuteness. Not recommended for beginners. Get at least two.

—*Anonymous*

Cats don't like change without their consent.

—*Roger A. Caras*

A cat is the only domestic animal I know who toilet trains itself and does a damned impressive job of it.

—*Joseph Epstein*

Your cat will never threaten your popularity by barking at three in the morning. He won't attack the mailman or eat the drapes. He may climb the drapes to see how the room looks from the ceiling.

—*Helen Powers*

If toast always lands butter-side down, and cats always land on their feet, what happens if you strap toast on the back of a cat and drop it?

—*Steven Wright*

The cat could very well be man's best friend but would never stoop to admitting it.

—*Doug Larson*

Cat: A lapwarmer with a built-in buzzer.

—*Anonymous*

I am not a cat man but a dog man, and all felines can tell this at a glance — a sharp, vindictive glance.

—*James Thurber*

For a man to truly understand rejection, he must first be ignored by a cat.

—*Anonymous*

Curiosity killed the cat, but for a while I was a suspect.

—*Steven Wright*

No amount of time can erase the memory of a good cat; and no amount of masking tape can ever totally remove his fur from your couch.

—*Leo Dworken*

Most cats, when they are "out" want to be "in," and vice versa, and often simultaneously.

—*Louis J. Camuti*

Cats aren't clean. They're just covered with cat spit.

—*John S. Nichols*

Not as a bond-servant or dependent has this proudest of mammals entered the human fraternity; not as a slave like the beasts of burden, or a humble camp follower like the dog. The cat is domestic only as far as suits its own ends; it will not be kenneled or harnessed nor suffer any dictation as to its goings-out or comings-in.

—*Saki (H. H. Munro)*

If cats could talk, they would lie to you.

—*Rob Kopack*

A cat pours his body on the floor like water. It is restful just to see him.

—*William Lyon Phelps*

Essentially, you do not so much teach your cat as bribe him.

—*Lynn Hollyn*

I had been told that the training procedure with cats was difficult. It's not. Mine had me trained in two days.

—*Bill Dana*

There are people who reshape the world by force or argument, but the cat just lies there, dozing, and the world reshapes itself to suit his comfort and convenience.

—*Allen Dodd*

Cats are the ultimate narcissists. You can tell this by all the time they spend on personal grooming. Dogs aren't like this. A dog's idea of personal grooming is to roll on a dead fish.

—*James Gorman*

I think it would be great to be a cat! You come and go as you please. People always feed and pet you. They don't expect much of you. You can play with them, and when you've had enough, you go away. You can pick and choose who you want to be around. You can't ask for more than that.

—*Patricia McPherson*

No one can have experienced to the fullest the true sense of achievement and satisfaction who have never pursued and successfully caught a cat by his tail.

—*Rosalind Welcher*

Never hold a dust buster and a cat at the same time.

—*Kyoya*

If you want a kitten, start out by asking for a horse.

—*Naomi*

In order to keep a true perspective of one's importance, everyone should have a dog that will worship him and a cat that will ignore him.

—*Dereke Bruce*

It is in the nature of cats to do a certain amount of unescorted roaming.

—*Adlai Stevenson*

In the middle of a world that has always been a bit mad, the cat walks with confidence.

—*Roseanne Anderson*

Cats know not how to pardon.

—*Jean de la Fontaine*

It's better to feed one cat than many mice.

—*Norwegian Proverb*

Cats are possessed of a shy, retiring nature, cajoling, haughty, and capricious, difficult to fathom. They reveal themselves only to certain favored individuals, and are repelled by the faintest suggestion of insult or even by the most trifling deception.

—*Pierre Loti*

Cats seem to go on the principle that is never does any harm to ask for what you want.

—*Joseph Wood Krutch*

It's easy to understand why the cat has eclipsed the dog as modern America's favorite pet. People like pets to possess the same qualities they do. Cats are irresponsible and recognize no authority, yet are completely dependent on others for their material needs. Cats cannot be made to do anything useful. Cats are mean for the fun of it.

—*P. J. O'Rourke*

I like pigs. Dogs look up to us. Cats look down on us. Pigs treat us as equals.

—*Sir Winston Churchill*

If a cat does something, we call it instinct; if we do the same thing, we call it intelligence.

—*Will Cuppy*

Watch a cat when it enters a room for the first time. It searches and smells about, it trusts nothing until it has examined and made acquaintance with everything.

—*Jean Jacques Rousseau*

A man has to work so hard so that something of his personality stays alive. A tomcat has it so easy, he has only to spray and his presence is there for years on rainy days.

—*Albert Einstein*

By what right has the dog come to be regarded as a noble animal? The more brutal and cruel and unjust you are to him the more your fawning and adoring slave he becomes; whereas, if you shamefully misuse a cat once she will always maintain a dignified reserve toward you afterward—you will never get her full confidence again.

—*Bruce Schimmel*

A human may go for a stroll with a cat; he has to walk a dog. The cat leads the way, running ahead, tail high, making sure you understand the arrangement. If you should happen to get ahead, the cat will never allow you to think it is following you. It will stop and clean some hard-to-reach spot, or investigate a suspicious movement in the grass; you will find yourself waiting a fidgeting like the lackey you are. But this is not annoying to cat lovers, who understand and appreciate a good joke, even when it is on them.

—*Robert Stearns*

What if it was cats who invented technology, would they have TV shows starring rubber squeaky toys?

—*Douglas Coupland*

Dogs have owners, cats have staff.

—*Anonymous*

By and large, people who enjoy teaching animals to roll over will find themselves happier with a dog.

—*Barbara Holland*

Cats know how to obtain food without labor, shelter without confinement, and love without penalties.

—*W. L. George*

Cats will not tolerate rough handling, beating, or teasing. They dislike exceedingly to be laughed at.

—*Anonymous*

The cat always uses precisely the necessary force, other animals employ what strength they happen to possess without reference to the small occasion.

—*Philip Gilbert Hamerton*

A soft indestructible automaton provided by nature to be kicked when things go wrong.

—*Ambrose Bierce*

It has pleased many small boys to make scientific investigation into the proverbial saying that a cat has nine lives.

—*Anonymous*

It is remarkable, in cats, that the outer life they reveal to their master is one of perpetual confident boredom. All they betray of the hidden life is by means of symbol; if it were not for the recurring evidence of murder—the disemboweled rabbits, the headless flickers, the torn squirrels – we should forever imagine our cats to be simple pets whose highest ambition is to sleep in the best soft chair, whose worst crime is to sharpen their claws on carpeting

—*Robley Wilson, Jr.*

When the cat's away, chances are he's been run over.

—*Michael Sanders*

One is never sure, watching two cats washing each other, whether it's affection or a trial run for the jugular.

—*Helen Thomson*

Cats are a waste of fur.

—*Rita Rudner*

How to Outsmart Your Cat

CATPOETICS

The author has turned up so much poetry about cats that he includes it here only to demonstrate that he's researched cat books going back to he's not sure when.

A dog will often steal a bone,
But conscience lets him not alone,
and by his tail his guilt is known.

But cats consider theft a game,
And howsoever you may blame,
Refuse the slightest sign of shame.

When food mysteriously goes,
The chances are that Pussy knows
More than she leads you to suppose.

—Anonymous

Ye cats that at midnight spit love at each other,
   Who best feel the pangs of a passionate lover,
I appeal to your scratches and your tattered fur,
   If the business of love be more than to purr.

—Thomas flatman

Gather kittens while you may,
   Time brings only sorrow;
For the kittens of today

Will be old cats tomorrow.
—Oliver Herford

Men
Are like cats
It's not the smallest use their denying it.
They love sitting beside fires,
Dozing.
They worship food
With an unholy devotion.
They adore comfort,
And yet they will not yield their independence
For these things.
They purr when stroked
The right way
But they will only be loving
When they feel like it.
And they cannot be taught
Tricks.
They are jealous when in love
And also fickle.
They are independent, greedy, selfish,
Athletic when young, lazy, comfort-loving,
And yet so charming —
Just like cats.
—Mary Carn

You, who've rejected the pick of the dish
   And flatly refuse to be stirred
By the mention of meat if you know there is
   Or of fish if you know there is bird.
Who insist your sole be a la bonne femme
   And your chicken direct from the breast,
Who will only touch trout that is recently caught
   From the shadowy shoals of the Test,

You who drink nothing but Grade A
    And turn your nose up at fine grouse,
Will happily trifle and toy
    With any desperate mouse.

                —Anonymous

Two years ago if anyone
Had said I'd do what since I've done;
If anyone had told me that
I'd leave my chair to let a cat
Out of the house at seven-ten,
And rise to let her in again
At seven-twelve, and let her out
At seven-sixteen or thereabout,
And rise once more to weary feet
The whole performance to repeat
At seven-eighteen and -twenty-two
I should have answered, "Nerts to you!"
And "Nerts!" I should have sneered again
But that was then. Ah, that was then!

                —Baron Ireland

He blinks upon the hearth-rug
    And yawns in deep content,
Accepting all the comforts
    That Providence has sent.
Louder he purrs and louder
    In one glad hymn of praise
For all the night's adventures,
    For quiet, restful days.
Life will go one forever
    With all that cat can wish –
Warmth and the glad procession
    Of dish and milk and fish.

Only – the thought disturbs him –
    He'd noticed once or twice
That times are somehow breeding
    A nimbler race of mice.
—Alexander Gray.

When Noah beached on Ararat
He found that he had saved a cat
(Or rather two) from where the Flood
Had left the earth submerged in mud.
In getting up his list he'd winked
and tried to make the cat extinct,
Because he knew, and knew full well,
Its tendency of raising hell.

But somehow, in the rainy dark,
Two cats had sneaked aboard the Ark
And had triumphantly survived,
Malicious, sly, and many-lived.
"Ah, well! Said Noah, "that is that!"
And put a curse upon the cat,
A complex, triple-jointed curse
That can't be reproduced in verse.

So that is why the cat will play
And frisk and frolic all the day,
And lie beside the fire and purr,
And let the children stroke his fur,
But it remembers, after dark,
The curse it heard on Noah's Ark,
And sings, in ecstasy of fright,
A hymn of hate throughout the night.
—Stoddard King

How to Outsmart Your Cat

I like the simple dignity
    That hedges round the cat;
You never see her howling,
    She lets the dog do that.
You never catch her leaping hoops,
    Nor prancing on the floor
Upon two legs, when
    Dame Nature gave her four.
We train the dog to hunt the birds,
    And beat him when he fails.
He works all day, and never gets
    A single taste of quail.
A cat is wiser far than he,
    She hunts for birds to eat;
She does not run her legs off, just
    To give some man a treat.
All cats, no matter what their breed,
    Are born aristocrats;
They never, like the terriers, make
    A trade of killing rats.
The dog's man's servant, plaything, drudge,
    A foolish altruist;
The cat, in spite of man, remains
    Serene, an egotist.

—*Anonymous*

FAMOUS CATS

The very fact that some cats are famous says less about the cats than about their owners. So if you want your cat to be famous, get yourself famous first.

For instance, John Lennon's cat Charo did not achieve greatness by falling out the window of the couple's New York City apartment [splat]. It did fall out the window but it survived, earning itself a footnote in the Lennon story.

Here are some others:

Wuzzy, owned by writer Paul Gallico
Bismarck, Florence Nightingale's cat
Cuddles, kooky kowboy singer Kinky Friedman's
Chopin, Zelda and F. Scott Fitzgerald's Persian
Dweezil, Dweezil Zappa to Robert Wagner
Sprite, belonged to Bill Watterson
Puffins, US President Woodrow Wilson's cat
Calico, actress Joan Fontaine's gray Persian
Beelzebub, one of Mark Twain's cats
Blackie, Winston Churchill's cat
Blatherskite, yet another of Mark Twain's cats
Catarina, Edgar Allan Poe's cat
Taffy, belonged to Christopher Morley
Dolly, Tallulah Bankhead's Siamese cat
Chanoine, the cat of Victor Hugo
Sadie, a Siamese belonging to James Mason
Jellyloru was T. S. Eliot's cat
Columbine, writer Thomas Carlyle's black cat

Buffalo Bill, still another of Mark Twain's cats
Snowball, one of Ernest Hemingway's cats
Cuthbert, one of two black cats of P. D. James
Dancer, cat of Walter Cronkite....

Those were just the cats found in a whole bunch of cat books. I've since Googled "Famous Cats" and you know what? The Google people have Famous Cats out the wazoo. Hundreds of them. Way too many to bore people with. So the hell with it.

The stubborn belief of many dog lovers that cats are worthless is easily dispelled by stirring accounts such as this, in which a courageous feline's rescue work would certainly have earned it several columns had it not been forced to compete with Chicago's St. Valentine's Day Massacre.

THE VERY END

Our little cartoon cats have been stolen from "Fat Freddy's Cat" by Gilbert Shelton, who produced Frank Stack's "The Adventures of Jesus" in 1964 (the prototype of Underground Comix that thrilled the Hippies of yesteryear). Both Shelton and Stack are cronies of the author.

Provocateurs include Retired Speleologists Bob McClure, Don Goodson, Jerry Chastain (RIP), and Crime Writer Tamara Shaffer. Enablers include Sharon DiRago, Bill Towler, Claude Matthews, and Jenny-Lynn Ferrell.

Doctor Naismith was cooked up in 1966 as founder of The John Dillinger Died For You Society and has since been featured in many other literary projects.

Plus Floozie the Cat and Anonymous.

AS FOR THE AUTHOR...

Sherlock Holmes in Chicago / Page 5
Vegas electronic show roundup / Video
Kehr on Mel Gibson's 'Hamlet' / Take 2

Bill Helmer is a former *Playboy* editor, wrote books on gangsters and outlaws of the 20s and 30s, but mainly wants to be remembered as the guy who, in 1969, parlayed his master's thesis into the first history of the Thompson submachine gun—*The Gun That Made the Twenties Roar*. He does not approve of firearms developed after WWII, however.

His recent books include *John Dillinger: The Untold Story* (1994), *Baby Face Nelson: Portrait of a Public Enemy* (2002), *The St. Valentine's Day Massacre* (2004), *The Complete Public Enemy Almanac* (2008), and *Al Capone: Memoirs of a Mobster's Wife* (2013).

Bill is a member of the Discordian Society, the Bavarian Illuminati, and a Founder of The John Dillinger Died For You Society. He was once a Spelunker, Amateur Radio operator W5AJR, and a staff member of the National Violence Commission.

He wants to be a fireman when he grows up.

112 Harvard Ave #65
Claremont, CA 91711 USA

pelekinesis@gmail.com
www.pelekinesis.com

Pelekinesis titles are available through Small Press Distribution, Baker & Taylor,
Ingram, Gardners, and directly from the publisher's website.

CPSIA information can be obtained
at www.ICGtesting.com
Printed in the USA
JSHW080037051122
32624JS00001B/6

9 781949 790740